ALL THE LOST YEARS

BY JOANNE RYAN

Copyright © Joanne Ryan 2021

Tamarillas Press

All Rights Reserved. No part of this publication may be reproduced or transmitted in any form or by any means, electronic or mechanical, including photocopy, recording, or any information storage and retrieval system, without permission from the author.

This book is a work of fiction. All characters, locations, businesses, organisations and situations in this publication are either a product of the author's imagination or used factiously. Any resemblance to real persons, living or dead, is purely coincidental.

Cover artwork: Canva

Design: © Joanne Ryan

ISBN: 9798753032560

CHAPTER ONE

I waited until nearly three o'clock so that I could be absolutely sure that the next door neighbours had gone out. They've usually gone to work by half-past-eight but even knowing that it had taken me all day to muster up the courage to go outside.

As I stepped out onto the doorstep I quickly realised that I'd made a terrible mistake because I could see that their battered Land Rover was still parked on their driveway, which meant that Derek, at least, was still at home. Just my rotten luck that this was the one day he deviated from his routine. I shouldn't have assumed they'd gone but short of hanging out of the front door I couldn't know for sure. The driveways are set back from the front of the houses making it impossible to see.

When I saw the Land Rover I wanted to run straight back into the house and lock the door but I gave myself a quick, stern talking to and forced myself to shut the front door firmly behind me and lock it.

I can't stay hidden in the house forever; I have to start facing up to things.

I managed to slip silently down the driveway and settle myself into the front seat of my car without being spotted. I was attempting to shut the car door without making any noise when it was rudely wrenched out of my hand and yanked fully open.

'Ave you seen my Snowy?' My next door neighbour's face filled the open doorway and he bellowed into the car at me without so much as a *hello*. Derek is a mountain of a man and his slightly effeminate lisp seems strangely at odds with his appearance. I have no idea how he'd managed to sneak up the drive without me seeing or hearing him. I took a deep breath in, taking care to breathe through my mouth so I couldn't smell his corned beef odour, and answered as calmly as I could.

'Snowy? No, I haven't seen him.'

He narrowed his eyes at me.

I stared back at him, determined not to break eye contact as this would confirm to him that I was lying.

'I ain't seen him since I let 'im out to do his business yesterday morning. Somefing must've 'appened to him,' he boomed.

'Oh dear,' I said, in what I hoped was a sympathetic voice. 'I'm sorry, Derek, I haven't seen him at all.'

He'd stared at me for a few more moments

and then straightened up and stared at the garage doors as if they would tell him where his dog was.

'If you see 'im let me know,' he bellowed down at me. 'Cos he'll be frightened, poor little 'fing.'

He then slammed the car door with force – luckily my fingers weren't in the way – and stomped off down the side of the driveway, trampling my log edging under his huge Doc Marten boots as he went. I took a deep breath, placed my hands on the steering wheel and gripped it tightly to try to stop my hands from shaking.

I know that I should confess to Derek and tell him the truth and take the consequences but I simply don't have the strength. I console myself with the fact that everyone in the street is afraid of Derek and his wife, Eileen, and that I'm only behaving in the same way that everyone else would.

This is a very nice street, in a 'good' area and Derek and Eileen simply don't fit in. There's no way they could've afforded to buy a house here and they're only able to live next door because they're renting. My friend and next door neighbour, Nancy, has had to go into a nursing home and her son decided to rent out the house to help pay the fees. Nancy is gripped in the jaws of dementia so she has no idea that her house is now being inhabited by 'the Clampits', as Douglas, my nephew, rather unkindly calls them. Nancy would be horrified if she could see the mess they've made of her lovely garden. I miss Nancy dreadfully; she'd lived in this street even longer than I have.

Derek and Eileen are very direct. No beating about the bush with social niceties or small talk, just straight out with whatever it is they want. Eileen has a particular way of looking at you that makes you believe that she knows exactly what you're thinking about her and she's well aware that it isn't complimentary. Everyone in the street also gives their son, Chester, a wide berth, as he's shaping up nicely to be a mini Derek. I've overheard Chester refer to me to his hoodie-ed mates as *the old bag next door.* It's true that I'm old, seventy last birthday, but I don't think I'm a bag. I did try to be nice to him when they first moved in, said *good morning* and *hello* but all I got back was a puzzled look and a snigger.

Snowy the dog isn't very nice either, small, rat-like and barky, he's not snowy at all but more of a dirty white. He has bald areas of missing fur where pink wrinkled patches of skin show through.

Snowy usually *does his business* as Derek puts it, on my front garden and Derek never picks it up, or apologises, or even acknowledges that it's my garden and not his. Strangely, Snowy never does his business on *their* garden.

I should confess, I know I should; but I just can't.

When the shaking in my hands had finally stopped, I looked in the reversing mirror to see Derek standing at the end of my driveway, arms akimbo, hands on hips, surveying the street for signs of his dog. I could hear him even though the door was shut, shouting *Snowy* in his booming, loud, lisping way.

If George were here now he'd know exactly what to do, he wouldn't be sitting here in a quivering state like me.

I shake the thought away and start the car up, put it into gear, carefully check in the mirror and reverse slowly down the driveway. I stop at the end with the engine idling until Derek eventually takes the hint and reluctantly moves aside so that I can reverse onto the street. I force myself to acknowledge him with a little wave as I sail off down the road. I can almost feel his eyes burning into the back of my head as I drive off. Or maybe I'm imagining it.

He'll surely be gone by the time I come back.

I *have* to go to the shops today because I've no food in the house and my nephew Douglas is coming to visit after he's finished work. He'll be expecting to be offered coffee and biscuits at the very least or else we'll have the *you're not looking after yourself properly, Auntie Ria* conversation again. We'll probably have that conversation anyway and also the *Power of Attorney* one but I'm certainly not going to give him any ammunition. Last week when he visited I'd run out of milk and I thought he was going to have me whisked into an old people's home that very instant.

I *am* looking after myself perfectly well and if I run out of milk then I simply drink my tea black, but Douglas seems to think that I'm incapable of functioning without someone to watch over me.

Douglas thinks it would be much easier if I moved from the house into something more manageable. An apartment, Douglas thinks, would be ideal. This house is far too big, he says, and if I moved into an apartment I wouldn't have the bother of a garden. An apartment would be much *easier* now that George isn't here to look after me.

I've told Douglas on many occasions that I like doing the gardening but he doesn't listen. I was the one who ran the house and looked after the garden, not George, and if anything needed repairing or decorating, George certainly didn't do it; we got someone in and paid them. I don't bother telling Douglas any of this, because I've repeatedly told him and he never listens and I don't think he ever has. I just let him talk and get it all off his chest while I think about something else.

I concentrate on driving and try to forget about Snowy, Derek, Douglas, and the fact that I'm seventy-years-old and everyone seems to think that I'm old and past it. I don't think seventy is old at all; Helen Mirren is older than me and I'm sure no one would tell her she needs to go into a home or that she's unable to manage her own finances.

I don't *feel* old either; in fact eighty doesn't seem that old to me now that I'm only ten years away from it. I'm not being conceited when I say that I don't look my age; I could certainly give Helen Mirren a run for her money. My hair might be pure white but it's thick and wavy and I've kept myself trim. I certainly don't look or feel like a doddery pensioner.

George was two years older than me and no one would have had the nerve to suggest to him that he wasn't able to look after himself. I can imagine his outrage if Douglas had suggested that he needed to give him Power of Attorney, or that he should move into an apartment. Douglas wouldn't have *dared*.

I had intended going to Tesco's on the outskirts of town but in my haste to get away from Derek I turned left instead of right and now I'm on the way to the town centre. I may as well keep going because I can get everything I need from the Sainsbury's in the precinct.

I've driven all this way on auto-pilot and I wonder if I'd have even noticed if I'd run someone over.

I already know the answer to that one.

Concentrate, Ria, concentrate.

I pull in to the car park behind the precinct and park neatly between a shiny Jaguar and a brand new Audi. After feeding the ticket machine and putting the parking ticket on the car windscreen I head towards Sainsburys. I walk briskly through the entrance and straight along to the bakery section where I pick up a large crusty loaf and a couple of cream horns, Douglas's favourites. While he's eating them he won't be able to talk which will give me a break from the incessant nagging.

Not a nice way to talk about your only remaining relative, is it? Although to be absolutely correct Douglas is *not* my relative, he's George's. George's deceased brother's son. I don't have any living relatives left of my own, not one. And I know that Douglas is only trying to help but sometimes I wish he'd just shut up and go away.

What would Douglas say if I told him about Snowy? I'd probably have to tell him twice because he wouldn't be listening the first time. Once he'd actually heard what I was saying and recovered from the shock he'd probably want to move me out of the house immediately. Have me committed, most likely.

Because when I told Derek that I hadn't seen Snowy, I was lying.

I know exactly where he is.

He's hidden underneath some empty compost bags at the back of my garage.

And he's very, very dead.

✽ ✽ ✽

Douglas is tucking into his second cream horn; he ate the first one so quickly it can barely have touched the sides. I sip my tea and watch him devouring it and think how handsome he is, how very like George he is. George and Douglas come from a long line of good looking men and like George he's very clever and good at making money.

George was immensely proud of him; Douglas has worked and studied extremely hard and has a top job doing something very important. I don't know what the job is because no one ever tells me any details because they think that I'm far too dim and past it to understand.

Douglas lives in a rather grand, expensive house on the outskirts of town which has four bedrooms – all with en-suites – and a huge, beautiful garden which Douglas and his wife never use. They don't sit out in it, even in the summer, because the sun causes skin cancer and is not good for you. They pay a gardener to come in and mow the lawn and maintain it for them every week in the summer and once a month in the winter. Their house is beautiful and pristine, like a show home. It's so perfect that you wouldn't believe that anyone lived in it; when I'm forced to visit I feel uncomfortable for squashing the sofa cushions. It's also very cold because they never have the state-of-the art heating on because central heating isn't good for you, according to Prue, his wife. When I visit – which isn't very often, thank God– I always make sure to wear trousers and put an extra thick jumper on.

Douglas licks the last of the cream from his fingers before taking a swallow of his tea and I'm reminded of him as a little boy; he loved his food. We didn't see so much of him then but once George's brother died we became a lot closer.

Well, George did.

Douglas was a bit on the chubby side when he was a teenager but once he met Prue she put him on a diet and now there's not an ounce of fat on him. I'm positive that Prue would never allow a cream horn into their house. Or a chip.

'They were delicious, Auntie Ria. Although my waistline will probably regret it later.'

'Nonsense,' I say with a smile. 'Now and then doesn't hurt.'

Douglas drains his cup and from the thoughtful expression on his face as he places the cup carefully back on the saucer, I can tell what's coming next.

'Have you thought any more about setting up the Power of Attorney?'

'I'm still thinking about it,' I say.

Douglas frowns. 'I really think you should. It would prevent a lot of problems.'

'I'm only seventy, Douglas. I'm not quite senile yet, you know.'

He looks shocked.

'Of course you're not! I'm not suggesting that you are but it's best to have it in place.' He coughs. 'To prevent any problems if you do get, you know, a bit forgetful. Prue meets people all of the time who wish they'd had the foresight to set up a Power of Attorney.'

I bet she does. Prue works for the council and is some sort of social worker who 'assists' old people making the transition into a care home.

'I'll think about it,' I say.

'I'm only trying to help, Auntie Ria.'

'I know you are – and I do appreciate it. I just need some time to think about things. Take it all in. I'm still getting used to the situation.'

'Of course, of course.' He looks a bit uncomfortable, as well he should, because Douglas knew all about the state of mine and George's finances, whereas I've been kept in the dark for the last forty odd years. 'I just want to look after you now Uncle George isn't here,' he says. 'Make things a bit easier for you.'

For a minute I feel slightly ungrateful. I know he's only trying to help in his own way. It would be so easy to sit back and let him take care of everything and the old Ria would have done just that and been relieved that he was here to take control. I don't even know *why* I'm being so awkward; it's not as if I have any idea what to do with it all, it's far too much money for one person to spend.

The problem is, George wasn't supposed to die first, I was. I'm the fragile, delicate one and George was always the robust, healthy one and it was assumed that I would go before him.

A very young seventy-two, George still went to the gym three times a week and he looked and acted much younger than his age. It was a terrific shock for everyone when he had a heart attack nine months before he died and no one could quite believe it. Not that George was going to let a heart attack stop him from enjoying life; he followed the doctors instructions for rehabilitation to the letter and was soon back to his old self. The doctors thought it highly unlikely that it would happen again; he didn't even need surgery. So George going first has rather thrown a spanner in the works because that wasn't the way things were supposed to be and now I'm being difficult for no good reason.

The thing is, I don't want to be awkward but I can't seem to help it. It's not even about all of the money that I never knew that we had, I don't care about that; it's the lies.

Or rather, *the* lie.

'Have you decided what you're doing about Christmas?' I say, in an attempt to steer the conversation away from the power of attorney.

Douglas doesn't look up as he's totally engrossed in his mobile phone. He could, at least, pretend to listen, couldn't he? I'm almost tempted to tell him about Snowy to shake him up a bit.

'Christmas?' I say, a bit louder.

'Sorry?' he looks up from his phone in puzzlement.

'Have you and Prue decided what you're doing for Christmas? Are you going skiing?'

Douglas and Prue go skiing every year – apart from last year when obviously they didn't go because George died at the end of November and it wouldn't have been *seemly* for them to go on holiday, according to Prue. Last Christmas is just one complete horrific blur to me. I can barely remember any of it.

'Um, yes, we're staying at home, didn't want to leave you on your own at Christmas. We'll probably go skiing later in January. You'll be coming to us for Christmas day, won't you?'

This is what I feared. Call me ungrateful but I'd be more than happy to spend Christmas Day on my own with a Marks and Spencer Christmas dinner for one and a box set of *Call the Midwife*.

'Oh, don't worry about me,' I say. 'Christmas is just another day as far as I'm concerned. You go off and enjoy yourselves skiing, I'll be fine. I couldn't possibly expect you to miss your skiing again for me.'

Douglas looks horrified. 'Oh no, Auntie Ria, we couldn't do that, we couldn't enjoy ourselves knowing that you were here all on your own. Uncle George would have wanted us to take care of you.'

The prospect of Christmas Day with Prue and Douglas at Bleak House makes a care home seem almost attractive. Prue is on a perpetual diet and by association so is Douglas and anyone else who crosses their threshold. The thought of a calorie controlled, low-fat Christmas dinner in a freezing cold house is almost more than I can bear.

I'm well aware that Prue doesn't care much for me either, she speaks to me very slowly and loudly because she thinks that I'm mentally backward. She never knows what to talk to me about because I've never had a job since George and I got married and I've had *mental health problems*, as she likes to call them. It's not her fault, I was happy to let George do the talking for the both of us for most of my life. I never made much attempt to get to know her so is it any wonder that she thinks I'm a bit dim? Maybe I am a bit dim.

'You could come here?' I venture. At least I could have the fire on and cook something decent with fat and salt in it.

'Oh, no, we couldn't possibly put you to all that trouble.'

'It's no trouble, honestly,' I say. 'It would give me something to do, it's not as if I've got anything else to do and it's only fair because you and Prue both work so hard.' I'm warming to the idea now. I'd still rather spend the day on my own but if I have to see them I'd rather do it in comfort.

'I'll suggest it to Prue,' Douglas says uncertainly. I'm certain that Prue will say no because she won't be in control of the calories and I'll want to put the television on and watch something that isn't a documentary. But at least now we won't have to talk about it anymore today, a brief respite until Douglas's next visit. As a last resort I could always be ill; there's a lot of flu around at this time of year. I could wait until Christmas morning and then ring them and tell them that I'm not feeling well. It would probably work because Prue has a bit of a thing about germs, she's always washing her hands and sterilizing everything in sight.

'Yes, do,' I say, brightly. 'Now, can I get you another cup of tea?'

CHAPTER TWO

A loud banging noise wakes me. I lay in bed wondering what it could be and after listening for several minutes conclude that it's more of a hammering than a banging. A quick glance at the alarm clock on the bedside cabinet confirms what I suspect – because it's still quite dark and I have a job to see the numbers on the clock – it's only ten past seven.

Curious to know what all the noise is about I slip out of bed and pull my dressing gown off the hook on the back of the bedroom door and put it on. The heating doesn't come on until eight o'clock and the bedroom feels decidedly chilly. Perhaps I should change the timer to seven o'clock now that George is no longer here. Or maybe I should just leave it on for twenty-four hours a day, it's not like I can't afford it.

I slip my feet into my slippers and pad over to the window, lift the corner of the curtain and peer down into the street. In the gloom I can just make out the large, track-suited figure of Eileen from next door standing on the footpath in front of my garden. As I watch I can see that she had a hammer in one hand and is holding the top of my three-foot-high wooden fence with the other.

I watch for a while – leaving the bedroom light off so there is no possibility of her seeing me – and I see that she's definitely hammering something onto the fence. Small and made of wooden slats, the fence surrounds my front garden and serves no purpose except for decoration – but I still think it's a bit much that she thinks she can nail something to it without my permission. Although obviously I would have said yes if she'd asked, because Eileen's not the sort of person you say no to.

The thing she's hammering looks like a sheet of paper, or maybe card, which seems an odd thing to be attaching to my fence. I wonder if it's some sort of Christmas decoration, because we're into December now and I know that some people like to put their decorations up early. Maybe it's a nice picture of Santa or perhaps a Christmas tree. Which is a ridiculous thought because Eileen would hardly bother to decorate my garden fence, would she?

And as I dismiss this thought as stupid my heart starts pounding, because I suddenly think that maybe she's nailing up a sign that says *dog murderer*. I quickly realise that this is an equally ridiculous thought because Eileen doesn't yet know that Snowy is dead.

And it was actually an accident, not murder.

I honestly didn't *mean* to kill him and I felt quite sick when it happened. I'm simply not capable of deliberately hurting an animal and even though he was a horrible little dog, he was their pet and they obviously loved him.

I was simply doing what I do every morning, without fail, come rain or shine – getting the car out of the garage and parking it on the driveway so that it was ready to use. That's my daily routine; get up, have breakfast, get showered and dressed and then go and drive the car out of the garage onto the driveway.

It was something that George did every single day when he was alive and I've carried on his routine. He insisted that the car was garaged every night and got out first thing in the morning so that it was ready on the drive, all shipshape and Bristol fashion - George's words, not mine. Sometimes the car would sit there all day and not be used at all but it still had to be got out, just in case it was needed. The process would then be repeated in reverse in the evening and the car would be put back in the garage for the night.

I'm not doing it anymore after what happened, the car can stay in the garage unless I'm going out. Or better still, I won't even put it in the garage in the first place, I'll just leave it out on the drive all of the time and then it's always ready.

If George was still here then Snowy would still be alive because he wouldn't have allowed the next door neighbours' dog to roam around on our driveway on his own. George would have *had a word* with Derek the very first time that Snowy *did his business* on our garden and would have told him that he had to keep him under control on a lead. Derek would have complied willingly with George's request, because people always did what George asked them and then Snowy wouldn't have been running loose and he wouldn't be dead. George had a certain way with him and people tended to do what he asked. He was never rude and always asked very nicely and politely and somehow, it seemed deeply unreasonable to refuse him anything.

I'm doing that *thing* again; since George has been gone I start thinking about things and one thought leads to another and before I know it, whoosh, an hour or two has gone by and I can't remember what I was thinking about in the first place. Maybe that's what I was doing when I killed Snowy – not concentrating. It's quite possible but I really can't remember very clearly.

I feel quite relieved that I don't have to un-garage the car every day anymore and just wish that I'd thought of not doing it sooner and then Snowy would still be alive and I wouldn't have a dead dog in my garage.

That morning was like any other, I'd unlocked the garage doors (wooden, hinged, not the new fangled up and over metal type which George *would not give house room to*), got into the car, started it up and reversed out onto the driveway.

I've replayed the event over and over in my mind and I *think* I can recall hearing next door's back door slam, so they'd obviously let Snowy out *to do his business*. But it didn't really register with me at the time because my next door neighbours are unable to close a door without slamming it so I've become used to their noisiness and tend to ignore it.

As I was reversing the car, the back end bumped up and I realised with a horrible sinking feeling that I'd hit something. Maybe it was an uneven paving slab or a stone, I tried to tell myself, but I knew, really, that it wasn't.

I stamped my foot onto the brake pedal even though I wasn't going fast at all and stopped the car and pulled the handbrake on. I opened the door and climbed out and walked around to the back of the car praying that I was wrong, but of course I wasn't.

Snowy's feet were poking out from underneath the car and they weren't moving.

I felt sick and my stomach rolled and I thought I was going to vomit up my breakfast right there on the driveway. I forced myself to breathe in and out through my nose slowly to stop myself from getting dizzy and after several moments I slowly bent down to have a look underneath the car. I was quite certain that Snowy's head was going to be all squashed and bloody with brains splattered everywhere and I wished I could just go indoors, climb into bed and stay there and pretend it had never happened. It took me back to how I felt just after

George died; absolutely horrific and as if I was in some sort of waking nightmare.

But, to my astonishment, there wasn't a mark on that dog, not one. His head was in front of the wheel, just touching it, but there wasn't any blood, not even the tiniest bit. Before I could talk myself out of doing it I grabbed hold of his feet and pulled. I must have pulled a bit harder than I intended because he came right out from underneath the car so fast that I had to step back so he didn't land on my feet. I bent down and made myself lay my hand on his chest to see if he was breathing and although he was still warm his chest wasn't moving at all. His tongue was lolling out of one side of his mouth and his eyes were open and staring at me so I knew he was dead. And I *did* feel terrible, because although he was a nasty mutt I *do* like dogs and I'd never deliberately hurt one. I would have liked a dog myself but George wouldn't countenance it, he said that they were too much trouble and we wouldn't be able to go on holiday so much. He said this every time I suggested a pet and when I said that there lots of dog kennels who could accommodate our holiday needs he said that actually, he was a bit allergic and dogs made him sneeze so, that was that.

Anyway, there I was, standing in front of a dead Snowy (I'd like to say that he looked peaceful in death but he didn't, he still looked rat-like and nasty looking) and I quickly realised that I'd either have to confess what I'd done to Derek and Eileen or hide the evidence.

Confessing was never really an option, because I couldn't see Derek and Eileen saying *you killed our dog? Not a problem*. No, I'm quite sure that I'd *never* be forgiven and they'd have put a contract out on me or something, so I hurried back into the garage and looked around for something that I could use to pick Snowy up. I should have picked him up with my bare hands but I didn't want to touch him again, which is stupid really because he was hardly going to hurt me.

I stood in the middle of the garage and my hands were shaking and I couldn't see anything because of my panic. Luckily the old coal shovel was leaning against the wall at the far end of the garage so I couldn't really miss it and I hurried across to get it. We don't have a coal fire anymore, we have a modern gas fire that turns on at the flick of a switch, but the coal shovel is very useful for when we get snow.

Or for picking up dead dogs.

I picked up the shovel and rushed out to the car with it, praying all the time that Derek or Eileen didn't come out of their house because there'd be no excuse in the world that would explain why I had their dead dog on a shovel. I attempted to scoop Snowy onto the shovel but it wasn't as easy as I thought it would be and I only succeeded in pushing him back underneath the car. I had no choice but to touch him again, so I grabbed hold of his feet with one hand while I slid the shovel underneath him with the other. As soon he was on the shovel I picked it up and almost ran back into the garage. Once inside I laid the shovel down on the floor before pulling the doors closed behind me.

I leaned back against the doors and heaved a big sigh of relief and I came over all light-headed and saw stars dancing in front of my eyes for a moment. I'm not sure how long I stayed like that, it could have been ten seconds or ten minutes, but the sound of Derek and Eileen's back door opening brought me back to my senses. I held my breath as I listened to the sound of Derek's boots tramping up their driveway while he called out for Snowy.

I froze rigid, too afraid to even move. In my panic I realised that I'd left the car engine running. Would Derek notice and think it strange? Would he somehow guess what had happened? What would I do if he knocked on the garage door?

The thought of Derek opening the garage door spurred me into action and I picked up the shovel and crept on tiptoes to the end of the garage so that my heels wouldn't make a noise on the cement floor. I laid the shovel down taking care not to make a noise, and pulled some empty compost bags that I'd kept to put garden rubbish in over Snowy to cover him up. I knew that at some point I'd have to make a decision about what to do with him but that would have to be done later, when I was calmer. The thought of digging a grave in the back garden or having a bonfire and putting him on it popped into my head and I tried to shake the image from my mind because the thought of Snowy's body burning made me gag. I had to take a deep breath and compose myself before I went back and slowly opened the garage doors. As I stepped outside Derek was standing there looking at my idling car in puzzlement.

'Morning Derek', I managed to say, wondering if he'd notice how odd I sounded.

He looked at me and then looked at the car.

'Gloves,' I pronounced, pulling my gloves from my pocket and waving them at him as if they were vital evidence. 'Forget my head if it wasn't screwed on.'

He grunted something which I didn't catch and then he turned and stepped over the low wall separating our driveways and stomped off into his back garden. I waited until I heard the slam of their back door and then I reached into the car and turned the ignition off, closed the car door and went back into the house. I left the key in the ignition and didn't even lock the car I was in such a state. The car sat like that on the driveway until the next day so anyone could have stolen it.

So that's the whole sorry episode of how Snowy died and neither Derek nor Eileen has any idea that their pet is no more.

The hammering has stopped and I watch as Eileen lumbers down the street and proceeds to hammer a sheet of paper or card to a telegraph pole. I think that maybe it's a lost dog poster but I'll know for sure when I go out later on.

I'm going to have to decide what to do with Snowy's body. He's been dead for a couple of days now and I can't leave his body in the garage forever. It's fortunate that it's winter otherwise he could be going off; I'm not sure how long it takes a body to start decomposing and I've no wish to find out.

I can't hide away in the house forever so I'm going into town to get my Christmas shopping done even though Christmas is still three weeks away. I know that if I don't make myself go out today, I'll succumb to the fear and hide away forever and I'll have to be dragged from this house kicking and screaming.

In my nightie, most likely.

It'll be easy shopping as I know exactly what I'm going to buy; a jumper from Marks and Spencer for Douglas and a bottle of perfume for Prue. Christmas present shopping completed. I need to get on with things and stop dithering and try to act as if I haven't killed my next-door neighbour's pet.

When I come back from shopping I'm going to go out to the garage and wrap Snowy in a bin liner, put him in the boot of my car and drive to the council tip. I've been to the tip before and chucked away household rubbish so I just have to drive up the ramp and park and throw Snowy over the barrier and into the skip with all of the other unrecyclable rubbish. I'm pretty sure Snowy's not recyclable and although I'm sure you're not meant to put dead animals in with the rubbish, what else can I do?

The sound of the letterbox clanging makes me jump and I let the net curtain drop and step back from the window as I catch a glimpse of the postman walking back down my garden path. Half-past-seven, he's keen. I watch him walk along the front of the garden and then disappear up next door's driveway. I can't help feeling impressed that he hasn't taken a short cut over the garden wall. He's wearing knee-length shorts even though it's December.

I walk over to the bed and pull the duvet back and give it a good shake and fold it over the end of the bed to let it air and then make my way downstairs. A quick bite to eat, into the shower and then off into town to beat the morning traffic. Hopefully my favourite car park won't be full which will mean I can avoid having to park in the multi-storey. As I get to the bottom of the stairs I stop on the bottom step and stare at the post that's just plopped through the letterbox and landed on the doormat.

Just one letter.

Printed and official looking.

I didn't think it would arrive so soon.

❉ ❉ ❉

It's half-past-three by the time I drive up the ramp of the multi-storey car park. It's far too late to get a space in my preferred car park due to my time-wasting today.

So much for getting here early.

I got distracted again; *whoosh* and hours and hours had gone by, just like that. I fully intended going shopping in the morning but foolishly thought I could quickly look at something on the computer and before I knew it practically the whole day had gone. I spent far longer than I intended in George's study on the computer; I never looked at it at all when George was alive but I'm slowly learning. Actually, not so slowly, as unbelievably, I seem to have an aptitude for it. I bought one of the *PCs for Dummies* books and I'm gradually getting to grips with finding my way around everything.

I should have done it years ago.

Here I go again; thinking too much and now I've gone and driven up ramp after ramp on autopilot and I'm on the top floor. A quick glance confirms that every single parking space is empty and I wonder if I should drive back down to a lower floor. Would I be safer on one of the lower, more crowded floors where there are other people about? Is the top floor a mugger's paradise, is an opportunist thief just waiting for a lone woman to arrive so he can rob her?

No, I decide, why bother driving down to the lower floors and searching for a space to park when there are so many spaces up here. I need to be a bit braver, a bit more Helen Mirren, I remind myself. I pull into a space in the middle row and am turning the ignition off when a movement at the side of the car park catches my eye. As I get out of the car I see that there's a large holdall pushed up against the corner wall with a dog sitting on top of it. The dog is tied to the handle of the holdall with a piece of string attached to its collar and is looking very sorry for itself.

Medium sized with tufty, tan fur, he looks bedraggled and cold. I stand next to the car and scan around the car park for the owner of the holdall and dog. There are no other cars at all, only mine.

Maybe this is a test, my conscience suggests, to see if I really like dogs as much as I say I do.

'Shut up!' I say crossly. Aware that I'm now talking to myself – surely the first sign of madness – I immediately feel embarrassed when I realise that there's a girl sitting on the wall in front of the dog and she's likely heard me. I don't quite know how I missed her before and can only think that she must have only just sat down.

Not the best place to sit as she has her back to me which means that her legs are dangling over the side of the wall – six storeys up. Taking a deep breath and without thinking about it too much, I hitch my handbag over my shoulder and march towards her. I can't ignore the fact that there's a girl sitting on a wall in a dangerous position six storeys up. I walk briskly towards her but don't call out to her in case I startle her and she slips off the wall and plunges to her death. As I get closer I veer over to the left so that I'm approaching her side on which will mean that she'll see me coming.

The dog starts barking and makes me jump as I get closer but the girl doesn't move at all. I stop a few feet away from her and noisily clear my throat but I'm not sure if she can hear me over the barking.

'Quiet, Rocky!' She doesn't turn around as she speaks and the dog gives a final, squeaky bark before settling back down on top of the holdall with his head between his paws.

'Your dog's very well trained,' I say, to her back.

She turns her head slightly to the side but I can't see her face as the wind whips her long hair around her head.

'Look,' she says. 'I'm not being rude but I'd rather be left on my own if you don't mind.'

Her fair hair is very long and a gust of wind wraps it across her face and she takes one hand off the wall and pulls her hair to one side. I take a step forward and then stop myself. I have a horrible feeling that she's going to jump, because I can't think of any good reason why someone would sit on a wall so high up.

'Aren't you cold sitting up here?' I say. 'Your dog's shivering.' As soon as I've spoken I could kick myself. She could be suicidal and the best I can come up with is to ask her if she's cold.

She doesn't answer, just shrugs.

'Is there someone I can call for you? Your parents? A friend?'

She laughs but there's no joy in it.

'I don't think so,' she shouts, without turning around.

'A friend?' I suggest, realising that I'm completely out of my depth and have no idea what to do. George would know what to do if he were here.

'Nope.'

I stare at her and desperately try to think of something to say.

'I'm Ria,' I say. 'What's your name?' Honestly, is this the best I can come up with?

'Kayla,' she says flatly, turning her head towards me slightly.

'How old are you? Kayla?' Perhaps if I keep her talking I can stop her from doing something stupid because the more I think about it, the more I think she's going to jump. Why else would she sit with her feet dangling over the edge?

'Seventeen.'

'Your parents,' I say. 'They'll be worried about you.'

'She won't. She's kicked me out.'

I'm shocked that someone could throw their seventeen-year-old out onto the streets.

'Where are you living?' I ask, in an attempt to keep her talking.

'Nowhere. The social worker put me in a place but they won't let Rocky stay. I smuggled him in but they found out so I had to leave.' The words come in a rush and she continues staring straight ahead as she speaks.

'Maybe I could ring your mum for you?' I suggest. 'Whatever's happened I'm sure you could sort it out. She'll be very worried about you.'

'No!' she almost shouts, the wind snatching her words from her. 'She's made her choice. I'm NEVER going back there and she wouldn't have me anyway.' The last word comes out on a sob and I wish I knew what to say.

'Look,' I say. 'Why don't you get off the wall and we can go and sit in my car and talk about things, it'd be much warmer and I'm sure we can work something out.'

'No. I'm staying here,' she says. 'I'll be alright. You can go.'

I move a little closer, wondering what on earth I can do. Should I call the police or will that just make things worse?

'What about your friends?' I ask. 'Could you go and stay with one of them?'

She gives a snort. 'Yeah, course, I'll give them a ring and ask them to get the spare room ready.' She turns her body slightly so she can look at me and it hits me how very young she is. 'No one wants to know and even if they did I can't take Rocky with me.' Her voice catches on the last few words and I see her throat bob as she swallows down the tears.

'Why don't you get down from the wall?' I say, gently. 'We can sort something out. Nothing's ever quite as bad as it seems.' I know this isn't true even as I utter the words because wasn't there a time when I longed to end it all myself?

She shakes her head and takes one of her hands off the wall. Oh God, what do I do?

'You can't jump,' I say quietly. 'Because Rocky will be on his own. Who'll look after him then?'

She doesn't speak and takes her other hand off the wall and pulls her hand back from her face. I want to reach out and grab her but I'm afraid, I'm terrified that she'll leap to her death and I won't be able to stop her.

'What about,' I say, inching closer. 'If you had somewhere to stay and you could keep Rocky with you – would you get off the wall then?'

She shrugs again and I want to scream at her not to keep shrugging because she's going to overbalance and fall.

'Not going to happen, is it?' she says. 'No one cares. Apart from Rocky no one in the whole world gives one shit about me.'

I'm inches from her now and I hold out my hand towards her.

'I care,' I hear myself say. 'You and Rocky can come and stay with me.'

CHAPTER THREE

'Yeah, right, Kayla says. 'I know what'll happen. As soon as I get off the wall you'll start coming up with excuses. That's what people do, make excuses.'

'I won't,' I say. 'I promise. You and Rocky can stay at my house for as long as you like.'

She turns her head slowly and narrows her eyes and looks at me with suspicion.

'But why?' she asks. 'Why would you help? You don't even know me.'

Why, indeed. I said it because I thought she was going to jump to her death and I wanted to stop her. I can't take it back now. Although there's no reason why she can't stay with me, I have plenty of room and no one to consider except for myself. Except for Douglas and Prue, of course. They won't like it.

'Someone helped me once, when I was your age,' I say, in what I hope is a convincing manner because it's a complete lie.

She doesn't move.

'Please.' I try to make my voice stronger, more convincing, more Helen Mirren. 'Get off the wall. Come and stay with me and we'll sort things out.'

I hold my breath.

'You promise that Rocky can come too?'

'I promise. He absolutely can.'

She stares into the distance and then moves one leg to swing it over the wall and her whole body wobbles and for one horrible moment I imagine her plummeting to her death. I lunge forward and grab hold of her arm and pull her towards me and she falls backwards onto her holdall. Rocky yelps and scrambles out from underneath her in a jumble of legs and paws.

'Ow!' Kayla screams. 'What did you do that for?'

'Sorry,' I say, helping her to stand up. 'I thought you were going to fall and I didn't want another death on my hands.'

❋ ❋ ❋

So I never did get to Marks and Spencer to get Douglas's jumper but I did meet a seventeen-year-old girl called Kayla who for some reason that I can't understand myself, I have promised a home to.

And her dog.

I manhandled Kayla's enormous holdall into the boot of the car while she settled herself in the front seat and hauled Rocky onto her lap. I got into the driver's seat and turned the heater on full blast and drove home. It was very quiet while I was driving and when I stopped at the traffic lights and sneaked a glance at her, Kayla's eyes were closed and her head was nodding. The dog was snoring too.

They're still asleep when we arrive home and I pull the car onto the driveway and turn the engine off. I touch Kayla gently on her arm and say her name but she doesn't stir. After repeating her name until I'll almost shouting I have to resort to gently shaking her when she doesn't stir. She wakes with a start and looks at me in wide-eyed alarm.

'Sorry. I couldn't wake you,' I say.

'Wha...?'

'I'm Ria, remember? You and Rocky are going to stay with me?' She looks at me as if I'm mad and then realisation slowly dawns on her. Her face is an open book and I see the emotions flitting across her face; confusion, relief and then suspicion. She's trying to understand what my motives could possibly be and then I see her visibly relax when she reasons that I'm ancient and a woman so therefore, no real threat at all.

'Sorry,' she says, dipping her head as she strokes Rocky. 'It takes me a while to wake up properly.'

'That's okay. Let's get inside in the warm.' I open the door and get out and Kayla opens her door and Rocky lollops out onto the driveway and Kayla follows him. She comes around to the back of the car and once I've opened the boot, drags her huge holdall out and we trundle into the house.

It's lovely and cosy as we step into the hallway because I left the heating on high whilst I was out – a little luxury that I allow myself now that I have control of the finances and the thermostat – and I usher Kayla and Rocky into the lounge.

'Make yourself at home and I'll get us something to eat. What do you fancy?' As I say it I realise that the choice is very limited as I have hardly have any food in the house. One of the drawbacks of living alone is that if you buy lots of food most of it ends up in the dustbin.

'Anything.' Kayla stands still and looks around the lounge taking in the patterned carpet and wallpaper and mahogany furniture. It must all seem hideously old-fashioned and museum-like to her.

'I'll eat anything,' she says. 'Can Rocky have a bowl of water?' She sits down gingerly on the sofa and Rocky plonks himself down on top of her feet.

'Of course,' I say, picking up the television remote control. 'I'll put the TV on for you.' I have the television on all day and every day as I can't bear the silence but I rarely watch it. I turn the TV on and hand the remote control to Kayla and go out to the kitchen.

I pull open the fridge door; eggs, bacon, butter and a hunk of cheese stare back at me. I'll need to go food shopping now I have a house guest but for tonight bacon, egg, baked beans and some crusty bread will have to suffice. I wash my hands and then get the frying pan out of the cupboard and put it on the hob to heat up. I open the packet of bacon and debate how many rashers to cook. After a moment's consideration I decide to cook all of them because I'm sure that Rocky will gobble up anything that's left over.

I open the packet and lay all of the rashers in the pan and while they're sizzling I set about finding a bowl to put some water in for Rocky. It's a fruitless search as I have nothing suitable, no plastic tubs or metal bowls, nothing dog-like at all. Although I do have a very nice pottery salad bowl that we bought in Cyprus on holiday many years ago. It's about the right size and has a large base so won't tip over. It was expensive and I used it a lot in our dinner party days but I never use it at all now. I'm not likely to have any dinner parties in the future, am I? It'll do, I decide, and if it gets broken it doesn't matter because I never use it anyway. I fill the bowl with water and place it on the floor by the back door.

I have a kitchen full of nice things, all expensive and top of the range because George would never have anything cheap. Most of them sit unused in the cupboard and when I'm dead what will happen to them? They'll go to the nearest charity shop or down the council tip. I don't have anyone to pass them on to and I'm sure that Prue will turn her nose up at anything of mine.

George would be furious if he could see that bowl being used for a dog bowl – which is a stupid thought because if he was here then Kayla and Rocky definitely wouldn't be. I wonder what George would have done if he'd been with me in the car park; would we have walked over and asked her if she was okay? We definitely would because George would never ignore someone who needed help, although there's no way Kayla and Rocky would have been allowed to come home with us. George would never have even considered that and neither would I because George would have thought I'd gone mad if I'd suggested it. He'd have sorted everything out in his usual efficient way – most likely he'd have called Social Services to deal with Kayla – and then we'd have continued with our shopping trip and that would have been that.

He'd be convinced that I'd gone completely insane if he could see me now, inviting a perfect stranger into my home. I can hear him in my head and know exactly what he would say; *you know nothing about her, she could be a thief or worse.* She could be for all I know but I don't actually care.

Maybe I have gone mad, or maybe I've finally woken up after a long, long time.

I turn the bacon over and leave it to cook while I cut slices of bread and spread them with butter. I put one on my plate and two on Kayla's and then add another to hers as I think she looks like she needs feeding up. Would she drink tea? A lot of youngsters don't, it's all fizzy pop and smoothies these days, or so the television tells me. I wouldn't know because apart from Kayla I haven't spoken to anyone young for a very long time. I don't have anything other than tea or coffee so I fill the kettle and put it on to boil; it's either tea, coffee, tap water or milk. Does anyone drink milk nowadays? I shouldn't think so. I open a tin of beans and plop them into a saucepan and put them on the stove to heat and then pile the bacon to one side of the frying pan so I can fry the eggs.

I'm humming the theme to *Emmerdale* as I potter around the kitchen and I realise I'm enjoying having something to do. I miss having someone to look after and cook for.

We could sit in the dining room to eat but that seems rather formal. There's the kitchen table but I think it'll be cosier if we eat in the lounge. George would never countenance eating a meal from a tray on his lap and I imagine his horror if he were here now. I rummage around in the larder until I find an old wooden tea tray that's seen better days. I also find a metal tray with *a present from Blackpool* printed in fading black letters over a picture of the tower. I have no idea where that came from as I don't remember ever going to Blackpool. Maybe it was George's mother's, I often used to find things that I'd never seen before and I assume that they came from her.

Or maybe I have been to Blackpool and bought it myself during the forgotten years; those years that I don't *want* ever to remember. I'm certain that I've been to places and given the appearance of actually living during the years that I have no memory of. I push the thought aside and wipe the dust from the trays with the dishcloth.

No point in thinking about that now.

I carefully dish up the bacon, eggs and beans onto the plates and arrange the knives and forks next to them on the trays. I look down at the trays and decide that it's not a bad makeshift meal considering that when I left the house I had no idea that I was going to have a house guest.

When I take Kayla's tray into the lounge she's sitting on the sofa engrossed in *Midsummer Murders*.

'Wow, that's smells lush,' she says, as she takes the tray from me and puts it on her lap. She has deep, dark circles underneath her eyes and her skin is so pale that it's almost grey. I wonder how long she's been sleeping rough because she looks absolutely exhausted. When I go back out to the kitchen and return with my own tray she's already eaten a slice of bread and a good amount of the beans although Rocky's licking his lips so I think that maybe he's had some too.

'This is amazing,' she says, between mouthfuls. 'Thank you so, so much.'

'You're very welcome,' I say as I settle myself down on the chair opposite her. 'Rocky can have the scraps when we're finished but I'll get him some dog food tomorrow when I go shopping.'

'What? You'd buy him food?' Her forks hovers mid air and she stares at me in disbelief.

'Of course,' I say. 'I'd hardly ask you to stay and

not feed you. I'll pop down to Tesco's in the morning.'

'But, you know, I haven't got any money or anything. I won't be able to pay you.' She shoves a forkful of fried egg into her mouth and looks down at her plate and I see that she's struggling not to cry.

'Don't be silly, you're my guest,' I say. 'I don't expect you to pay me.'

'But I can't expect you to feed me,' she protests. 'I don't know why you're being so nice to me; you don't even know me.'

'We all need a little bit of help now and then.' I put my knife and fork down on the tray. 'I'd like to think that someone would help me if I needed it. I'm paying it forward or whatever it is you youngsters say nowadays.'

She nods and makes a show of looking at the television.

'I love *Midsummer Murders*,' she says, in a wobbly voice.

'Do you?' I ask, surprised that a seventeen-year-old would like one of my favourite programmes.

'Yeah,' she says, through a mouthful of bread. 'I wish I lived there, it's lush. I wouldn't even mind getting murdered if I lived there.'

✽ ✽ ✽

When we've finished eating I persuade Kayla to stretch out on the sofa under the furry throw and have a nap. She doesn't put up any argument and

I've no doubt that the combination of a full stomach, a warm room and the thrum of the television will mean she'll soon be fast asleep. It's dark outside already and I pull the curtains closed and switch the lamps on, giving the room a warm glow.

Rocky follows me out into the kitchen and puts his nose in the air and sniffs. He must be hungry and the smell of the bacon will be tormenting him because he didn't get much in the way of scraps. Kayla and I both cleared our plates and I surprised myself with how much I ate. I have rather got into the habit of not bothering to cook as it hardly seems worth the effort for one. I usually just have a slice of toast or a sandwich.

I rummage around in the larder for something for Rocky to eat. I pick up a tin of baked beans and put them down again; not a good choice because they could lead to a nasty accident. I spot a tin of tuna nestling at the back and pull it out. I must have bought it for George as he loved tuna but I never eat it as I hate it. Rocky can have it. I open the tin and scrape the contents into a cereal bowl and place it on the floor beside the bowl of water.

As I watch Rocky gobble up the fish I realise that I've put the tuna in George's favourite cereal bowl; the one with pictures of golfers painted all around the outside.

I wonder if I subconsciously gave it to Rocky on purpose but quickly shake the thought off; of course I didn't. Why would I do that? George was the perfect husband and an absolute saint for the way he looked after me, everyone was always saying so. They didn't say it to me, obviously, but I'm not stupid, I know that was the general opinion. I've overheard too many whispered conversations and seen too many pitying looks to not know what people thought of me. Even our own friends, or rather George's friends, thought that I didn't deserve him. I saw the sly looks that George's friend's wives directed at his handsome profile at dinner parties; how unfair that he chose to stay with dull little me when he could have had someone like them. I knew what they were thinking; there aren't many men who'd have stood by their wife like he stood by me for all of those years.

With never a word of blame, not one.

Rocky finishes the tuna in seconds and I open the back door and let him out into the garden and watch as he circles the lawn until he finds a suitable spot. He seems well house-trained so fingers crossed, we won't have any accidents. When he's finished I let him back in and follow him as he trots into the lounge and flops onto the floor in front of Kayla with a sigh. Maybe he's tired too.

I leave them in the lounge and go back into the kitchen to tidy up. I open the dishwasher and load it up with the dirty plates and pots and pans and realise that I've hardly use it since George died. I've resorted to washing up in the sink because it would take me days to fill it up and the food would harden on the plates and then it wouldn't wash properly. It's still not full but I put it on anyway, I think I'll be using it a lot more now.

I go upstairs and across the landing into the largest of the two spare bedrooms at the rear of the house that look out over the back garden. Although there's a double bed in here, the desk underneath the window is full of George's paints and canvases because he had intended using it as a sort of studio but never really got round to it. With his golf and the club committee and all of his other hobbies there were never enough hours in the day.

It's a big room and the large desk in front of the window is perfect to catch the natural light. I open the desk drawer, where a few pens and a notepad rattle around. I put my arm in front of everything and sweep all of the brushes and paints from the top of the desk into the drawer. Most of the tubes of paint have never even been opened. I take the blank canvases from the top of the desk and stack them neatly underneath the desk.

I make up the bed with fresh sheets and turn the thermostat on the radiator up to the maximum setting. The mattress might be cold so I go back downstairs and root around in the kitchen larder – I call it the larder but really it's just a huge cupboard – until I find the hot water bottle inside a furry cover that Prue bought me a couple of Christmases ago.

I fill the kettle and while it's heating I fill the hot water bottle with cold water to check that it doesn't leak. It seems water-tight and there's absolutely no reason why it shouldn't be but I'd hate for it to leak all over the sheets.

When the kettle boils I carefully fill the bottle and take it back upstairs and place it in the middle of the bed under the duvet so it'll warm it up. I then go out onto the landing and open the airing cupboard and take a couple of towels out and take them into the main bathroom and hang them on the towel-rail.

I hardly ever use this bathroom, I always use the shower in my en-suite and only very occasionally will I use this bathroom if I want a bath. There's soap in the dispenser on the basin and shower gel and bubble bath on the side of the bath, so if Kayla wants a bath it's all here ready for her.

I look at my watch to see that it's a quarter to nine. I wonder if Kayla's still asleep. I debate waking her up and telling her that I've made her room up if she wants to go to bed. I feel awkward and unsure what to do because it's a very long time since I've had a house guest and I've never had one in such strange circumstances. I decide to make a cup of cocoa and use that as an excuse to wake her.

I go back downstairs and put the kettle on again and make the cocoa. I hope she likes cocoa; she drank the tea without any problem so maybe she will. Kayla's mumbling in her sleep when I go into the lounge and the smell of the cocoa makes Rocky jump up from his position next to her and this disturbs her and wakes her.

I put the packet of custard creams that I found lurking at the back of the carousel cupboard onto the coffee table . Even though we've eaten a meal only a couple of hours ago we've soon devoured the entire packet between us. Rocky enjoys them too and I'm sure a couple of human biscuits won't do him any harm now and then. I'll add dog biscuits to the shopping list for tomorrow.

Although Kayla's been asleep her eyes are beginning to droop again so I tell her that I'll show her where her bedroom is and it's up to her when she wants to go to bed. She admits that she's worn out and can't wait to get a good night's sleep. Without further delay we head upstairs.

'This is your bedroom,' I say, opening the door into the back bedroom. 'I've put a hot water bottle in your bed to warm it up a bit because the room's not been used for a while. The bathroom's next door and I've put you some towels in there.' I stand awkwardly inside the bedroom doorway and try very hard not to feel like a guest house landlady.

Kayla looks around the room and walks over to the window and pulls the curtains aside to look over the garden.

'I don't know what to say,' she says, in a forlorn voice.

'You don't need to say anything,' I say. 'You get a good night's sleep and you'll feel a lot better in the morning. Are you sure you don't want to ring your mother or anything? You can use my phone.'

'No.' A flash of anger crosses her face. 'Thank you.'

'If you're sure.' I back out of the door and start to

close it behind me.

'Ria?'

'Yes?' I pop my head back around the door.

'Can you leave it open, the door? I don't like sleeping with the door shut.'

I open the door wide.

'And Ria?'

'Yes?'

'Thank you for everything and for letting Rocky sleep up here. He's not used to sleeping on his own.'

I look at Rocky stretched out on the end of the bed and he raises one eyelid and looks up at the sound of his name.

'No problem, just make sure you both get a good night's sleep.'

Kayla flops down on the bed next to Rocky and puts her arms around him.

'We will,' she says, sleepily. 'Good night.'

'Goodnight, see you in the morning.'

I go back downstairs and sit on the sofa for a while and pretend to watch television. I don't want Kayla to think that I'm spying on her so I'll wait until she's gone to bed before I go back upstairs. As I sit back and put my feet on the pouffe and think back over the events of the day, the warmth of the room makes my eyelids start to droop.

I wake with a start and when I look at my watch I see that I've been asleep for over an hour. I get up and turn the television off and plump the cushions on the sofa. I collect the cocoa cups and take them out to the kitchen and put them in the sink and fill them with water.

I feel exhausted – it's been quite a day. As I climb the stairs I stop myself from looking in Kayla's room to see if she's asleep. She doesn't need me checking on her because she's not a child.

Although she seems like a little girl to me.

I pad lightly across the landing so I don't wake her if she is asleep and go into the en-suite to get ready for bed. Am I mad to offer a perfect stranger a home? George would definitely think so. But she has nowhere else to go and she needed help and the only way it seemed I could help her was by offering her a safe place to stay. I feel good that I'm able to help her, able to make up in some small way for killing Snowy, even though it was an accident.

To atone for my sin.

My *sins*.

CHAPTER FOUR

When I wake up it takes me several moments to remember that I have a house guest. I lie underneath the warm duvet and run through the events of yesterday. I have to ask myself if I'm going to regret bringing Kayla home with me: am I going to realise that I've done something really stupid that I can't get out of?

I lie still and mull it over and wait for the regret to hit; it doesn't.

I don't regret it at all, I decide. I'm glad that I offered her a home for however long she needs it. Who knows what would have happened to her if fate hadn't made me drive up to the top floor of the car park? It's true that I don't know her, but I don't think she's going to murder me whilst I sleep or steal from me. And I'm not just helping Kayla, she's helping me too, although she doesn't know it.

I know George definitely wouldn't approve and Douglas won't either. In fact, Douglas will probably use this as proof that I've finally gone completely ga-ga and will no doubt try to have me declared unfit or insane.

Too bad, I tell myself, feeling uncharacteristically brave.

I get out of bed and go straight into the en-suite and turn the shower on. I strip off my nightie and step into the shower and as I stand under the hot water I feel a new sense of purpose. I have a house guest – two if you count Rocky, and they need looking after and I'm the one who's going to do it. I'll see what I can rustle up for breakfast and then I'm going to write a shopping list and go to Tesco's and buy lots and lots of food.

Maybe Kayla would like to come too.

❋ ❋ ❋

Kayla looks much better this morning; her skin has the slightest hint of colour and the dark circles underneath her eyes don't look quite so severe. She's washed her hair and it hangs wet around her face making her look about ten years old. I'll lend her my hairdryer after breakfast otherwise she'll catch her death if she goes outside with dripping hair.

I didn't want to wake her because I thought she must be exhausted but as I was coming downstairs after my shower she was coming back up them with Rocky, who'd just been out in the garden.

She asked if it was okay if she had a bath and I

said of course it was and there was no need to ask. She spent a good half an hour soaking in there and then she came down into the kitchen for breakfast. We've just finished our breakfast of cornflakes followed by boiled eggs and soldiers which Rocky seemed to enjoy too.

As I was getting the breakfast ready it struck me that Kayla must be in some sort of education because she's only seventeen and I'm sure I read somewhere that nowadays youngsters have to stay at school until they're eighteen. I didn't want her to think that I was questioning her so I didn't mention it whilst we were eating but I feel that it's important. I attempt to find out in what I hope is a casual manner.

'Are you at college or anything?' I ask, as I write my shopping list.

'Yeah. College.' She shrugs.

'What sort of course are you doing?'

'Art.'

'Are you enjoying it?'

'S'okay.' She shrugs again.

I feel as if I'm pulling teeth but I need to know. I feel responsible for her although I don't want her to think that I'm interrogating her.

'So what days do you go to college?' I ask. 'Every day?'

'Yeah.' She shrugs again. 'Mostly afternoons. But I haven't been this week.'

Which makes total sense, because she's hardly going to go to college if she's homeless and thinking about ending it all.

'Doesn't hurt to have a little break,' I say. 'You can start fresh next week.'

She shrugs again. 'It's not worth it, there's only one more week and we break up for Christmas anyway. Not that Christmas is going to be any good this year.'

'What about last year, what was last Christmas like?' I say, in an attempt to stop the gloom descending.

Her face brightens. 'Brilliant, me and Mum always have a real tree and make our own decorations. We trim up the lounge, the kitchen and even my bedroom. At least we used to, not anymore.' Her shoulders slump.

'You and your mum might be able to sort things out – get back to how you used to be,' I offer.

'No,' she says, loudly. 'It won't ever be the same because of HIM. I hate him, he's an absolute pig but Mum can't even see it. She said I'd always come first with her but that's a lie. Since he turned up I can't do anything right.' She sticks out her bottom lip and it strikes me how very young she is.

'How long has he been around?' I ask.

'Since Easter. I quite liked him at first but he was just being nice to me so he could move in and take over.'

'When did he move in?'

'October. And it didn't take him long to show what he was really like. Disgusting pig.' Kayla bites her lip and looks down at her lap.

'What did he do?' I ask, but I think I know.

'Doesn't matter.' Kayla wipes her hand over her face. 'She doesn't believe me. I don't want to talk about it anymore.' I can see her throat bobbing as she holds back the tears.

'Right,' I say, changing the subject. 'How about we get this shopping list sorted so we can go and get some food in because we can't feed Rocky on cornflakes and eggs forever.'

Kayla nods without speaking and as we slowly add items to the shopping list she composes herself.

'Now,' I say, as we finish. 'How about you go and dry your hair and while you're doing that I'll clear up the kitchen.'

'I can help, let me do it, I'll wash up.'

'No need, I'll stick it all in the dishwasher. Besides, I need something to do otherwise I'd just sit around all day and go senile.' I stand up. 'Come on upstairs and I'll get the hairdryer for you.'

I go up the stairs and when I come out of my bedroom with the hairdryer Kayla's waiting on the landing.

'Thank you,' she says, as I hand the dryer to her. I turn to go back downstairs to clear up the kitchen but Kayla lingers on the landing.

'Everything okay?' I say, with my hand on the banister. Obviously everything's not okay but I don't know what else to say.

'Ria?' She looks at me uncertainly. 'Yesterday? What did you mean when you said you didn't want another death on your hands?'

* * *

We're on our way to Tesco's and I think everything is okay. Kayla didn't run screaming from the house calling me a murderer when I told her about Snowy. I said I felt really guilty about it because I like dogs, I really do. She said it was obvious that I was a good person because Rocky has taken to me and he's a good judge of character. She said he never took to HIM (her mum's boyfriend) which just proves that Rocky *knows.* I must admit that I felt quite choked when she called me a good person.

And the truth of it is that when she asked me about *another death on my hands* I got a bit confused and for a horrible moment I thought she knew.

Which shows that maybe I am going a bit senile because no one could possibly know.

It's just my guilty conscience.

Kayla says that obviously we can't leave Snowy's body in the garage forever and we need to get rid of it as soon as possible. I told her about my plan to take him to the tip and chuck him over the side and she agreed that was probably the best way. She said that she'd come to the tip with me if I wanted her to. I felt such relief when she said that, I'm so grateful that I don't have to do it on my own. We're not going today, though, because today is for shopping and buying lots of nice food.

I then asked her how she was feeling and if she felt that she needed to speak to a professional about her near-suicide attempt yesterday then I would do my best to arrange something for her. I felt that I had to ask because who knows what might be going on in her head. She looked at me in bewilderment and said that she had absolutely no intention of killing herself and asked whatever had given me that idea. I said that perching on a wall six storeys up with your feet dangled over the side is a very dangerous place to sit. She collapsed into peals of laughter and said she had no fear of heights and often went there to sort stuff out in her head.

I felt enormous relief when she said that she wasn't suicidal but I did make her promise not to sit on the wall in the future because she might accidentally fall.

I also told her how I'd been on my own since George died and she was speechless when I told her how long we'd been married – forty-six years – she said she couldn't imagine being with the same person for that long. I told her that when I was her age I couldn't imagine being as old as twenty-one as one year seemed like a lifetime but the older you get, the quicker time goes by. I shut up after that because I didn't really want to talk about George so I said we'd best get to Tesco's before it got too busy.

We arrive at the enormous, newly extended Tesco's, and to prove that I'm not a batty old lady

I park as close to the shop as possible. This means that I have to fit between two parked cars, instead of my normal habit of parking as far away as possible so I have at least four spaces to manoeuvre into. I make a fairly decent job of it and after Kayla gets a trolley from the dozens parked in front of the store, we march purposefully through the huge sliding doors into the supermarket.

Kayla is pushing the trolley around the aisles and it makes such a change from the little basket that I normally have. I find myself putting stuff in that's not on the list because I keep seeing things and thinking *well, that'll be nice* and of course Rocky needs a few squeaky toys to make him feel at home and some doggy treats too because he's been such a good boy. I can see that I'm going to have to buy some more shopping bags because it's obviously not all going to fit into the two *bags for life* that I've brought with me.

Kayla has explained that she should be able to get some sort of benefit because she's living away from home and going to college. I've told her not to worry about as it'll all come out in the wash – I had to explain to her what that meant – what I didn't say was that I've got more money than I know what to do with so it's not exactly a problem.

It still feels a bit odd knowing that I'm actually very rich because for years George has been telling me that we can't afford things. I wanted to go on a world cruise and have a new three-piece suite but George said we couldn't afford it so it was a bit of a shock to discover that I can now buy pretty much anything I want.

It's not that we didn't have lots of nice holidays because we did, it's just that they always centred around golf courses. George wasn't a mean man; far from it, but I've slowly come to realise that we only ever bought something if *he* wanted it and went to places that *he* wanted to go to. I didn't realise this for a long time because George was extremely clever at making me think that something was my idea when, in fact, it was his. And whatever we bought was always the best quality, we never bought rubbish, and I can't say that I ever wanted for anything because I didn't. But, having said that, I did tell him quite a few times how I'd like to go on a world cruise. I'd watched a television series about it and it looked so relaxing and different to our usual holidays and it really appealed to me. But whenever I suggested it his answer was always the same; it was too expensive and we had to make our money last so we could enjoy our retirement in comfort. He would then add that of course, if I really wanted to go we could, but that would mean that we'd have to limit our other holidays. I knew that he loved his golf so I felt mean then; I was being selfish by demanding a cruise when it would mean that he'd be denied playing golf.

Obviously, the truth of it was that he didn't want to go on a cruise because there are no golf courses in the middle of the ocean.

I'd still be in the dark about the money now if Douglas had his way. I can still remember the look on his face when I told him that I intended learning how to use George's computer. There was shock in his expression and also a hint of amusement. How could someone like me possibly find my way around a computer, his expression seemed to say, and really there was no need to worry my silly little head about it because he'd taken over from George and would sort everything out for me.

But I didn't want everything sorted out for me, I'd had forty-odd years of having everything sorted out for me and I didn't want any more of it, thank you. And that's how I found out just how well off we were because everything was very neatly documented on George's PC, including how to access online banking. I had already learned how much money we had because obviously it was all in the will, but I didn't take it in when the will was read because I was in such a state of shock. If I hadn't seen it in black and white on the computer, I don't think I'd have realised quite how wealthy I am.

One of the biggest shocks was how much money my parent's house had sold for. It was nearly twenty years ago and I shouldn't blame George too much because when Mum died, I was relieved that he took charge of everything and left me to grieve in peace.

I was heartbroken when Dad had died five years

before Mum but somehow it was even worse when she died; I felt that part of my life had gone with her and that no one, not even George, would love me the way they did.

So it wasn't his fault that I took no interest in the house sale but I *do* remember him telling me that the house was very old-fashioned and needed lots of work to update it and not to expect much when it was sold. I don't recall him telling me how much it sold for but I'm pretty damn sure that a hundred-and eighty-thousand-pounds wasn't mentioned.

One-hundred-and-eighty-thousand-pounds.

That was a lot of money nearly twenty years ago.

It would have bought a lot of cruises.

I'd never have know about it if I'd let Douglas take over everything – and perhaps I'd have been better off not knowing because I can't say that it did me any good finding out.

'Anything else?' Kayla asks, bringing me back to the present.

'No,' I smile. 'I think we've got pretty much everything.'

Kayla looks at the full-to-the-top trolley and laughs and heads towards the checkout. As she starts to unload everything onto the belt I go to the other end of the checkout and wait for the shopping to arrive.

Kayla puts through three new bags for life on top of the shopping – I hope that's enough – and the woman on the checkout, who doesn't look much younger than me, scans them and passes them to me.

'You've got the right idea letting your granddaughter do the hard bit,' she says, with a smile as she looks over at Kayla unloading the shopping onto the conveyor belt.

I'm about to correct her but I stop myself, I could have had a granddaughter if things have been different. And anyway, it's none of her business, I don't need to explain myself to a checkout operator.

'Wear the young ones out first,' I answer, with a smile.

I load everything into the carrier bags and when Kayla has emptied the trolley she joins me. Once we've finished packing the bags I pay for the shopping and we load the bags back into the trolley and walk out to the car park. Kayla is pushing the trolley, which is very full. I can't remember when I last bought so much.

'Have you got any grandchildren?' Kayla suddenly asks.

I shake my head. 'No. I don't have any children.' So she heard what the checkout operator said.

'So you're on your own?'

'Well, yes, I am. Apart from Douglas of course.'

'Who's Douglas? Your boyfriend?'

'No.' I laugh. 'He's my nephew, he was like a son to my late husband.' With a jolt I suddenly remember that he'll be coming to visit on Sunday and I'll need to think up some reason as to why Kayla's staying. I already know that he won't like it.

'Right,' she says.

'You must have grandparents, Kayla. Are you close to them?'

'No, not really, they live miles away, can't remember the last time I saw them. Mum doesn't have much to do with them 'cos she left home when she was really young. You're the only old person I know. Sorry,' she adds. 'I didn't mean to sound so rude.'

'That's okay,' I laugh. 'I am old, you're only stating the obvious.'

'It's funny though,' she says, turning to look at me. 'Because I thought old people were sort of a different species, you know, like from a different world but you're not, you're normal, you know, just like me.'

I can't help laughing and I laugh so much that Kayla joins in. We're still laughing as we reach the car and I click open the lock on the boot. Kayla insists on loading the bags and then she takes the empty trolley and pushes it towards the trolley park in the corner of the car park while I get into the car and start it up. I'm still chuckling to myself as I pull my seatbelt on and I realise how good it feels to laugh again.

It feels normal.

If only that were true.

* * *

The fridge is full to bursting and the cupboards have more food in them than they've had in years. Rocky has wolfed down his first proper meal of dog food and biscuit and is now happily playing with the blue and white striped whale that I bought him. It's making very un-whale squeaks every time he bites it.

We're making shepherd's pie for tea. Kayla is peeling potatoes while I chop onions. I've discovered that shepherd's pie is one of Kayla's favourite meals which is good because it's one of mine too. I haven't made it since George was alive because it's really not worth the bother of making it for one. Although I've only known Kayla since yesterday I feel comfortable in her company. I don't know whether it's because she's young or the circumstances of our meeting but I don't feel as if I have to pretend to be someone I'm not.

This is a new feeling for me.

We're chopping and peeling in companionable silence with Radio 2 on in the background and somehow, it just feels right.

'What sort of art are you studying, Kayla,' I ask, stepping back from the chopping board. I blink my eyes rapidly to dispel the tears, those onions really are strong.

'Oh, a bit of everything, really. Mixed media, drawing, oil and watercolour painting and a bit of pottery too. I've even weaved some of my own cloth and printed onto it. Basically anything arty. My favourite is painting.' She puts the peeler down on the board and stares out of the window wistfully. 'God, wouldn't it be amazing if you could get a job doing something that you loved and you actually got paid for it?'

'Well, there's nothing stopping you,' I say. "I'm sure there are lots of careers involving art.'

'No.' She picks up the peeler and stabs it into the potato. 'I'll have to get proper a job when college finishes, probably in a factory or a shop. Or maybe an office if I'm lucky.'

'Why? If it's your passion and you go on to university won't there be lots of jobs you can aim for?' I ask.

'No.' She shakes her head. 'I've looked into it and I won't be going to uni, it costs too much. You can get grants and stuff but realistically it's not going to happen because I'd have to basically work for nothing to get any experience and I can't afford to do that, it's all about internships and they're for rich kids, not the likes of me.'

'That can't be right.'

She shrugs. 'That's the way it is.'

'You're very philosophical about it.'

'No point being anything else, is there?'

'If you want to do some painting,' I say, as I sweep the onions off the board and into the oil sizzling in the frying pan. 'There're lots of paints and bits and pieces in the desk in your room. Help yourself.'

'Really? You wouldn't mind?'

'Of course not,' I say. 'You'd be doing me a favour

because they were only going to go in the charity bag.'

'Wow, thank you, that'd be amazing.'

I feel pleased that they won't be wasted; I probably *would* have sent them to the charity shop. Or they would have stayed there until I died and then been thrown out with all of the other things that no one wants.

We potter around the kitchen and after I've fried the onions I add the mince and Kayla puts the potatoes on to boil. My mind keeps returning to the fact that Douglas will be visiting on Sunday and he won't be happy to find Kayla here. I don't know why I'm so sure of this but I am. If I tell him the truth about how she came to be living here he'll use that as proof that I'm going senile. I can hear his voice in my head, *you just can't invite complete strangers to move in with you, Auntie Ria.* I'm worried that I won't be able to stand up to him and Kayla will be thrown out on her ear. Or even worse, that Prue will involve one of her many contacts in Social Services and Kayla will be whisked into care, Rocky will be sent to the dog pound and I'll be committed to an old people's home.

I need to get my story straight before he gets here.

'You've heard me mention my nephew, haven't you?'

'Oh, yeah, the one you're not close to?'

'That's him,' I say. Kayla doesn't miss much, or was it that obvious?

'Well, the thing is,' I say. 'He's going to ask me why you're staying here and who you are.'

'Ye-ah?' She turns to face me.

'Well, I thought I'd say that you're renting a room under the student letting initiative, I've read about it in the newspaper. I'll tell him that I contacted the college to enquire and they're short of rooms so that's why you're staying here.'

Kayla is looking at me in puzzlement.

'Why?' she asks, with a frown.

'Well, because they're short of rooms for students.'

'No.' She shakes her head. 'I get that bit. Why do you have to tell him that?'

'Because he'll wonder why you're staying here.'

'Is this his house?' She looks confused.

'No, of course not, I say. 'It's my house.'

'So,' she says, slowly. 'Why do you have to explain anything to him? What's it got to do with him?'

CHAPTER FIVE

I never thought I was the maternal type and I had no overwhelming yearning to be a mother but back in the early seventies you got married and you started a family becasue that's what everyone did.

I'm not saying that I didn't want children, of course I did, but it wasn't such a big decision back then because it was the natural order of things and what pretty much everyone did. I never considered not *having children, it never entered my head because that wasn't the done thing. I suppose when I thought properly about having children it was always as a something vague that was going to happen in the future.*

As it turned out, George and I weren't married for very long before I fell pregnant and I remember feeling rather smug that parenthood came so easily to us. I was pleased and excited to tell everyone our news and I lapped up all of the attention. George set about painting the nursery and I attempted knitting some baby's matinee jackets and it all seemed very exciting even though I couldn't imagine actually having a baby.

When Stephanie was born it was after a very long labour that involved just me and the midwife. George was nowhere to be seen because husbands weren't en-

couraged to attend births then. That all changed quite soon afterwards, but when I gave birth to Stephanie it wasn't an option and even if it was, I'm not sure that George would have wanted to be there.

Once she'd finally arrived I just felt immense relief that it was all over and quite truthfully, I would have been happy to have a sleep before I met my new daughter. I didn't suggest this, obviously, and when the midwife placed Stephanie in my arms I looked down at the top of her head and a completely unexpected rush of love enveloped me. I'd never felt anything like it and it took me totally by surprise. I'd heard of people falling instantly in love with their babies but for some reason I never expected it to happen to me.

She had a mass of black hair – which gradually faded to white blonde by the time she was six months old – with enormous blue eyes and the longest eyelashes that I'd ever seen. I'd never felt anything like it and would gaze into her cot while she was sleeping and marvel at how perfect she was. George was equally besotted and after a week in hospital – which was the norm then – we brought our new daughter home.

She was such a good baby, sunny-natured and contented, and even though I was a nervous first-time mother and didn't have a clue what I was doing, she soon settled into a routine and slept through the night. Mum told me that sometimes babies pick up on your nervousness and anxiety; that they can sense when you're not sure of what you're doing and it can make them fractious and unsettled but Stephanie was such a good baby – even with my inept attempts at mothering.

I remember asking Mum how she knew what to do when I was born – did some people instinctively know how to be a mother? She laughed and said that no, no one really knows but you soon learn. Thankfully I slowly gained confidence in my abilities and I loved my new role as a stay at home mother

George was at the beginning of his career then, on the first few rungs of the ladder of what would become an extremely successful career. Financially we were lucky that I didn't need to work and nor did I want to. Very few women went back to work after having a baby in those days, only those with high-flying, well paid careers returned to their pre-pregnancy employment. It wasn't like it is now when everyone seems to return to work whether they want to or not and staying at home to look after your own children seems to be frowned upon.

I'd always enjoyed my job as a secretary but I had no yearnings for a career and was happy to spend my days looking after Stephanie. I was content to fully immerse myself in my role as a mother and wife to a successful, career driven husband. George was the provider; it would be his career that dictated how comfortable our life would be, not mine, and I was more than happy with that.

And if George expected his dinner on the table every evening then that wasn't being sexist, just practical. He had his job to do and a lot of studying too; he needed uninterrupted sleep and peace and quiet to revise for his exams. I didn't expect any help and nor did I want it, looking after Stephanie was my job and I loved it.

When I look back now I remember long sunny days of taking her to the park and pushing her on the baby swing, her falling asleep on me in the afternoons, her first steps, her first words, her first everything. Life was pretty much perfect.

When Stephanie was eighteen-months-old I became pregnant again and I was delighted. Although I told everyone that I didn't really mind if it was a boy or a girl, the pregnancy felt different than the first. I secretly thought, and hoped, that I might be carrying a boy. I was an only child myself and although I'd had a very happy childhood, like most singletons I'd always yearned for a brother or sister.

I really had the most perfect life and was the luckiest person in the world.

For a while.

CHAPTER SIX

Kayla and I are going to the tip today to dispose of Snowy's body. I did suggest that maybe it would be better to wait until Monday because it won't be as busy as on a Saturday but Kayla thinks the busier, the better; hiding in plain sight.

Also, Snowy has been in the garage since Tuesday and I'm a bit concerned that he might be starting to smell. Every time I let Rocky out into the garden he sniffs along the bottom of the garage door and whines so it's probably best that I don't put it off any longer.

The two of us are standing in the kitchen ready to leave. We're wrapped up in thick coats with hats and gloves on because it's bitterly cold outside. Kayla is wearing a multi-coloured hat with an enormous pom-pom on it that I knitted years ago but have never worn. I loved it when I was knitting it and thought that it would be ideal for countryside walks in the winter. When I'd finished it, I tried it on and showed it to George but he laughed; he joked that I was far too old to wear something like that and he wouldn't want to be seen out in public with me. He said he was joking but I knew he wasn't and I felt foolish for thinking that I could wear it so put it away in a drawer.

Kayla says it's very *in* at the moment so I've said that she can keep it. I have a black mohair skull cap affair on which always leaves my hair in a frightful mess, but needs must.

There's talk of snow – the *Beast from the East* is threatening a return – and I'm conscious that another reason we need to dispose of Snowy's body is in case we get snowed in and he's entombed in the garage forever. We did discuss burying him in the garden under one of the rose bushes, but dismissed the idea because there's always the possibility that one of the urban foxes could dig him up.

'Ready?' I ask Kayla.

'Yep.'

I step out into the hall and wait while Kayla pulls the kitchen door shut whilst trying to keep Rocky in the kitchen at the same time. We're not taking him with us for obvious reasons. As I'm about to open the front door she puts her hand on my arm and gives it a squeeze.

'Don't worry,' she says, softly. 'It'll be over and done with in no time and we'll be back home before you know it.'

I manage a weak smile and open the front door and a small part of me is pleased; she said *back home*, as if she belongs here.

Once we're outside I close and lock the front door and we walk past the side of the car and stand in front of the garage doors. I unlock the doors and open one side and we go in and I pull the door closed behind us. It's gloomy inside with only the weak light from the side window illuminating the space. Luckily the window looks out into my garden so there's no chance of anyone looking in.

After our eyes have adjusted to the lack of light Kayla follows me to the back of the garage. I take a deep breath and pull the empty compost bags off Snowy and we both stand looking down at him. I pull two dustbin liners out of my pocket and stare at them.

'How are we going to do this?' asks Kayla.

'I thought I'd just pick him up and put him inside but I'm not so sure now.'

'Why?'

'What if he's started to decompose and gone squishy?' I feel myself gag as I say it and I put my hand over my mouth. 'What if I pick him up and he's all floppy?' I feel sick.

Without speaking Kayla gently takes the bin bags from my hands and shakes one open and tucks it underneath her arm while she shakes the other one out. She then puts one bag inside the other, bends down and slides it underneath the shovel and Snowy and shuffles the bag along the length of the shovel until Snowy is fully inside. She then slides the shovel out, doubles the bag over and picks Snowy up. I watch mesmerised and try to forget that there's a dead dog inside.

'It's all good,' she says briskly. 'Let's go.' She turns around and walks quickly to the front of the garage and I follow meekly like a child. I step in front and pull the door open and Kayla steps outside and I follow. Kayla waits behind me while I quickly close and select the key to relock the garage door.

'Alright?' I hear Kayla say. I have my back to her so I can't see who she's speaking to but my hands start to shake as I try to get the key in the lock.

'Morning.' I recognise the lisping tones of Derek and detect a question mark in his greeting. I finally manage to lock the door and turn around to face him.

'Morning, Derek. How are you?' I say, trying my best to keep the wobble out of my voice.

'So-so,' he says with a sigh. 'Still can't find our Snowy. We've even put posters up.'

'Yes, I saw them. Oh dear, no sign at all?' I can't believe we're having this conversation while Kayla is holding poor Snowy's dead body in her arms. I feel my cheeks start to redden with guilt.

'No, nuffin.' He looks at Kayla. 'You haven't seen him 'ave you?'

Kayla shakes her head, 'No, sorry. I'll look out for him though.'

Derek bites his lip and looks sad. 'Your granny can tell you what he looks like. There's a photo of him on the fence there but the colour's worn off the photo a bit now.'

'I'll have a look. Good luck with finding him. Come on Gran, we'd better go or else we'll be late.' Kayla looks meaningfully at me and walks round to the passenger side of the car. I press my key to unlock it and walk over to the driver's side of the car but can't get in because Derek is standing in the way.

'Where are you off to?' Derek asks.

I look at hi m in panic. I've never known Derek to talk so much and for the life of me I can't think of a suitable answer.

'Funeral,' Kayla says, loudly. 'Old family friend.' She adjusts the bag-wrapped Snowy underneath her arm in a nonchalant manner.

'Oh.' Derek looks confused and moves out of the way and I open the door and get into the car. 'Didn't think they did funerals on a Saturday.'

'Oh it's a humanist one so they do them any old time, not churchy or anything like that,' Kayla says, with authority as she gets inside the car and slips the bag into the foot well. 'Basically, they see you off in a cardboard box.'

As I settle in my seat Derek is still standing on the driveway watching us and I wonder if he'll ever leave. Would it look really rude if I closed the door? I feel in an agony of indecision and am thinking that we're never going to get away when Kayla leans across me.

'See ya!' she shouts through the open door to Derek. 'Gotta go or we'll be late.'

Derek hesitates for a moment and then takes the

hint and turns and clomps off down the drive and I finally summon the courage to close the door.

I pull my seatbelt across me and snap it into the clip, take a deep, shuddering breath and start the engine. As I reverse slowly down the drive I find that I can't look at Kayla because I have a horrible feeling that if I do I'll start to laugh hysterically.

We pootle down the street and I turn onto the main road in the direction of the council tip.

'I feel a bit bad.' Kayla finally breaks the silence. 'A funeral was the first thing that came into my head, I don't know why. I wasn't making a joke about Snowy being dead or anything. I feel sorry for him, I know how I'd feel if I lost Rocky.' She looks down in the foot well at the wrapped package lying on the floor.

'I know, I feel awful,' I say. 'And they're still looking for him too. I wonder if I should just confess and put him out of his misery. At least he'd know what had happened and could stop searching for him.'

'I think it's a bit late to confess now,' Kayla says. 'But I can totally understand why you didn't tell him because where would you start? There's no easy way of doing it.'

'There isn't, and he's a bit scary as well, isn't he?'

'Scary?' Kayla sounds surprised. 'I don't think he's scary, a bit rough maybe, but he seems like a nice man.'

I'm about to disagree with her but then stop myself; have I misjudged Derek? He is rough and ready but that doesn't mean he's scary or horrible. If I think about it he's never actually said or done anything horrible to me, apart from letting Snowy do his business on my front garden and trampling my log edging and I don't think either of those were deliberate, just careless. I decide I'll have to think about this once we've disposed of Snowy. I may have to revise my opinion of my next door neighbours. I also feel that I want to make amends to them somehow for what I've done but I have no idea how. Maybe Kayla will have some ideas.

'So, do humanists really have funerals on Saturdays?'

'No idea.' Kayla laughs. 'But the bit about the cardboard box was true, one of my mum's hippy, green friends died and she got cremated in a cardboard box made out of recycled stuff. Didn't want any more trees to be wasted by having a proper coffin.'

I think about this and remember George's funeral, he had the most expensive, magnificent oak coffin with heavy brass handles and a brass plate on the top. I did wonder if they actually burned the coffins or tipped the bodies out and reused them because it seemed such an awful waste to burn something which was so beautifully made. It wasn't a question that I felt I could ask the undertakers at the time. Or any time, really.

I think I'll have a cardboard box when I go. Or maybe a couple of bin liners, it'll be a sort of poetic justice.

I pull the car into the entrance to the tip, or the Council Refuse and Recycling Centre as it likes to call itself these days. There's a complicated multi-lane queuing system in place and we inch along behind the line of cars in front of us. As we get closer to the refuse area a dark-haired burly man wearing a bright yellow hi-vis vest with a cigarette clamped between his teeth directs us into the next available space. There are four lanes in all and another yellow-vested individual is at the head of the lanes letting one car up the ramp as one car leaves the ramp on the other side. One in, one out.

I pull the handbrake on and turn off the ignition because I know we're in for a long wait.

'Maybe we should have bought another bag of rubbish with us,' Kayla says, thoughtfully. 'It might look a bit odd coming all the way to the tip just to throw a small bag away.'

It certainly will, I realise with a jolt. Why ever didn't I think of that before?

'Maybe we should go home.' I start the car up. 'I could go in and get another bin bag and fill it up with rubbish.'

The car in front moves forward and the hi-vis vest man waves me forward. I can't turn around, there's not enough room, the only way out is up the ramp and along the top and down the other side.

'It'll be alright,' Kayla assures me. 'After all, it's not as if anyone knows what's in the bag and they'll all be too busy getting rid of their own stuff to notice ours.'

This is true although there's no getting away from the fact that it's odd to come all this way for one bag that I could just put in the dustbin. But people don't visit the tip to look at what other people are throwing away, do they? They're more concerned about getting rid of their own rubbish.

Anyway, it's no one else's business.

We inch forward a car-length at a time and finally arrive at the ramp. I drive slowly up it and pull the car in front of the only empty parking space and reverse into it.

'How about we both get out, you open the boot and we'll pretend we have lots of stuff to get rid of?' Kayla suggests.

I look around at the other cars, every boot is open and some people have their doors open too. Bin bags and cardboard boxes are being pulled from cars along with broken furniture and old garden tools.

'Good idea,' I say, turning off the ignition.

I open the door and get out of the car and hurry to the back while Kayla retrieves Snowy from the floor. I squeeze past the neighbouring car where a woman is pulling a standard lamp from the back seat. I click open the boot and stare unseeingly into it and wait for Kayla to join me. The car next to us on Kayla's side has both doors open and has blocked the way with assorted bags, bric-a-brac and boxes.

'You're not throwing them away are you?' a

voice asks from behind me.

I turn to see an elderly man wearing a flat cap staring into my boot.

I look at him in confusion.

'Pardon?'

'Those.' He points into the boot at George's golf clubs, not his best set but a very expensive set, nonetheless.

I'd forgotten they were in there and am about to say *no* but stop myself. Really, what am I keeping them for? They've been in the boot since George died because I've never bothered to move them. They're a nuisance; I have to pack the shopping bags around them and I really can't think why I've left them there for so long. I could give them to Douglas but he already has George's best set. Suddenly, I want them gone and I realise it'll give me enormous pleasure to haul them over the side and watch them drop into the skip below.

'Yes I am,' I say. I begin to drag them from the boot but the flat-capped man puts his hand on the bag.

'You can't throw them away, that's criminal. Put them in the recycling shelter over there.' He points towards a ramshackle open shed affair with a corrugated iron roof. It's full of assorted sticks of furniture, bicycles and old vacuum cleaners.

He's right, of course he is. Someone could have use of them or most likely sell them. I should really take them to a charity shop.

But I don't want to.

I don't answer him but grab hold of the bag and start to drag it out of the boot.

'Give them to me and I'll take them over there for you.' Flat-capped man insists.

'No, it's fine.' I turn my back to him in a non-too polite attempt to get rid of him.

'Oh, I can't let you do that.' He grabs hold of the other end of the bag. 'You shouldn't be carrying heavy stuff like that at your age.'

We face each other over the top of the bag and I tighten my grip. At my age? How dare he? He must be nearly ten years older than me.

'No.' I yank the bag closer to me. 'It's fine.'

'I insist.' He pulls the bag away from me. Out of the corner of my eye I see Kayla casually toss Snowy over the side and a vision of his body plummeting downwards to the skip flashes in front of me. I could put the golf clubs back in the boot and we could leave right now, there's really no need to stay any longer.

'Let me put them in the recycling for you dear, there's no need to worry yourself about them,' flat-capped man insists.

Maybe it was the 'dear' that did it, I'm not sure, but I look at him with barely concealed loathing.

'No, thank you.'

I pull the bag out of his hands and drag it towards the barrier but he still won't take the hint and again grabs hold of the other end of bag. As we reach the barrier an awkward tug of war ensues.

'Let go,' I shout. I'm shocked at the loudness and

don't recognise my own voice. It doesn't sound like me at all.

'You *can't* throw them away,' he insists. 'Let me put them in the recycling area for you.'

'NO. I don't want them recycled; LET GO,' I shout even louder.

We glare at each other but he won't relinquish his grip. I feel enraged. How dare he tell me what to do; it's nothing to do with him and I can throw them away if I want to.

'It's okay, thank you. We can manage,' Kayla's calm voice interrupts from behind him.

'They need to go in the recycling, love,' he says, turning to her. 'Leave it to me and I'll take them over there.'

Kayla ignores him and grabs hold of the end of the bag that he's holding and gently inserts herself between him and the bag, forcing him to let go and take a step backwards. He looks shocked and hovers around, watching us.

'Now then.' She adjusts her grip on the bag. 'If we give it a good swing it should go over.'

I grip the bag tightly and hold on as we start to swing it.

'One...'

We swing it between us, the momentum growing each time and on the count of three we let go and the golf clubs sail over the barrier and hurtle down to the skip below. There's a muffled thud as they land on the pile of rubbish.

I can hear jabbering from flat-cap man and he

looks at us in horror as we climb back into the car. Yes, it was such an awful waste.

But it felt so very, very, good.

CHAPTER SEVEN

Douglas is coming today.

I'd be lying if I said I wasn't nervous about his visit even though I have my cover story ready. Yesterday's burst of bravado has gone – I don't even know where that came from – and I'm feeling a bit embarrassed about it now if I'm totally honest. I almost apologised to flat-capped man on the way out because he looked so distraught when we threw the golf clubs away; it was so wasteful. I did wonder if he wanted them for himself but quickly dismissed that thought because he must have been nearly eighty.

Kayla never asked me why I was so intent on throwing away a perfectly good set of golf clubs although she did say that sometimes things are too painful to keep. I expect she thought that the golf clubs were a painful reminder of how much I miss my late husband but that's not the truth. All of our lives and holidays revolved around golf and it wasn't until I was confronted by the sight of them in the boot – something that I see every time I open the boot lid but take no notice of – that I was hit by the realisation that I hated them and never wanted to see them again.

Golf dominated George's life and by association, mine too. I've spent countless uncomfortable evenings in the company of my fellow golf widows wishing the hours away. George and his chums would spend hours regaling each other with their golfing tales whilst I counted the minutes until we could leave.

Well now they're gone.

Good riddance.

At the very least I've saved some other poor woman from becoming a golf widow.

So. Back to Douglas's visit. He usually arrives around three o'clock, stays for the maximum of an hour and then leaves, duty done. It's just an hour, that's all, I'm sure I can fool him for an hour.

I've bought him his favourite cream cakes and I'm going to wait until he's eaten the cakes before I introduce him to Kayla. Kayla and I have agreed that Rocky is going to stay in the garden for this visit because I don't think Douglas could cope with a lodger *and* a dog.

Small steps.

I cook a nice roast chicken for lunch with all of the trimmings, with a homemade apple crumble for desert. I'd forgotten how much I enjoy cooking and it's nice to eat proper meals again instead of meals for one or my usual piece of toast or a sandwich. For a slip of a thing Kayla has a very good appetite and is very complimentary about my cooking. I'd forgotten how nice it is to be appreciated because it's been such a long time.

We've barely cleared the plates away and squared the kitchen before Douglas arrives with his usual impatient rat-a-tat-tat on the front door knocker. Kayla quickly scampers upstairs after putting Rocky out in the garden with his toys and I take a deep breath before going out into the hallway. Douglas keeps asking me for a front door key so *if anything happens to me* he can let himself in. I've managed to put him off so far because I feel that once he has a key that'll be the beginning of the end. I've no doubt that he and Prue would be letting themselves in whenever they feel like it and I'll have no peace or privacy at all.

I pull open the front door and give Douglas a wide, welcoming smile and invite him in.

'Smells good, Auntie Ria,' he says, as he walks past me into the lounge. 'Roast chicken?'

'Yes, and all the trimmings.' I close the lounge door behind us and settle myself in the armchair.

'Nice to see you're cooking proper meals for yourself,' he says.

I don't know why he assumes that I don't always cook for myself because I've never told him that I don't. He has, without realising it, given me the perfect opportunity to inform him of the fact that I have Kayla staying with me.

'Well, I didn't cook it just for me,' I say.

He looks surprised and also slightly uncomfortable. 'Oh, thank you, Auntie Ria, but Prue and I are eating tonight.'

'Oh, I didn't mean you,' I laugh.

Surprise flashes across his features again, swiftly followed by puzzlement.

'I have a lodger,' I announce, as he opens his mouth to speak.

'A lodger?' he echoes.

'Yes. A lodger. I've been accepted on the college student rent-a-room scheme and my lodger moved in on Thursday. A very nice young girl. Her name's Kayla.'

Douglas's mouth falls open and he gawps at me; he's in shock and is making no attempt to hide it.

'You applied to the college?' he finally manages to ask.

'Yes. Several weeks ago.'

'Really?' He frowns. 'You never said anything.'

'Didn't I? It must have slipped my mind.' And why should I tell you everything? Is what I want to say but I manage to stop myself.

'But why?' He leans forward, hands on his knees. 'Do you want a lodger?'

'I thought it would be nice to have some company and help a youngster out at the same time.' It's really nothing to do with him but I feel that I'm being interrogated and have to justify myself. I make sure to speak in a way that doesn't give him the slightest impression that I'm in any way asking his permission.

'But you don't know anything about this person you've invited into your house,' he blusters. 'You've basically given a perfect stranger access to everything in your home.'

I say nothing.

'I don't know what Prue's going to say about it,' he adds.

I don't know why I need Prue's approval. For someone who works in social care at the council she's not very giving or caring. I only hope that she doesn't take it upon herself to check up on the rent-a-room scheme because I'll be found out in no time at all.

'I would have thought,' I say, 'that Prue would fully approve. She's always saying that the general public have to be forced into helping the community or taking part in any of the council initiatives.'

I watch as Douglas attempts to think of a fitting response as to why I shouldn't have a lodger. I feel rather pleased with myself and have to stop myself from smiling.

'I just think, Auntie Ria, that it would have been better if you'd talked it over with us first.' Douglas leans forward and gives me an earnest look.

'What? So you could talk me out of it?' The words are out of my mouth before I've thought it through properly and I see Douglas's eyes widen in surprise.

'No, of course not!' Douglas colours slightly because he's lying; that's *exactly* what they would have done. 'We could have helped to make sure that you were matched with someone suitable.'

I give him a tight-lipped smile and get up from the chair and go over to the lounge door.

'I'll go and get Kayla,' I say, as I open the door. 'And you can meet her for yourself.'

❋ ❋ ❋

I close the front door on Douglas and heave a sigh of relief. Thank God he's gone and that's over with.

'That didn't go too badly, did it?' I say to Kayla as we go into the kitchen and open the back door to let Rocky in.

'No,' Kayla says quietly.

Rocky is sitting outside waiting patiently and his tail starts to wag frantically as he trots into the kitchen. He follows me over to the counter where I keep his dog treats and sits down and waits, his tail swishing from side to side. I give him a treat and it's swallowed in one gulp so I give him another which gets the same treatment.

'Slow down, Rocky,' I say, with a laugh. I feel suddenly light-hearted and the knot in my stomach that was there before Douglas arrived finally unravels.

I knew that Kayla would come across well to Douglas; she speaks well and he would have no reason to dislike her, she is the very opposite of a stroppy teenager. My own experience with teenagers is very limited, my most recent being with my brief acquaintance with Chester next door who is probably not a good example at all.

When Douglas asked her about her art course, Kayla's enthusiasm shone through. When he attempted to ask her why she was using the rent-a-room scheme I stepped in and stopped him, surprising myself with my bravery. I didn't want him interrogating her the way he does me, she doesn't have to explain herself to him. I told him that her reasons were private and that we had no need to know what they were. Douglas made no secret of the fact that he didn't like being told to mind his own business and I've no doubt that when Prue visits us she'll attempt the same line of questioning.

'Right,' I say, as Rocky waits in vain for more treats. 'Now that we've got that out of the way, what shall we have for supper?'

'Do you think,' Kayla asks, thoughtfully. 'That he'll get his wife to check up on me?'

'Of course not,' I lie, trying to prevent her from worrying.

'Really?' Kayla's eyes search my face and I find that I can't lie to her.

'She will,' I admit. 'Most definitely. Probably first thing in the morning, if I know her.'

'So then she'll know all about me and from what you've said about her she'll be straight round here to throw me out.'

'She can't throw you out,' I say. 'This is my house and I decide who stays here, not Prue.'

Kayla is silent. She pulls out a chair from underneath the table and sits down.

'What's wrong?' I sit down in the chair opposite and face her.

Kayla shrugs.

'Please, tell me.'

She lets out a big sigh. 'It's just that I like staying here with you and I don't want to leave. Rocky likes it here, too.'

'You don't have to leave,' I say. 'Whatever gives you the idea that you'll have to leave?'

'Your nephew. He doesn't want me here and when his wife finds out about me they'll make me leave. They'll *make* you get rid of me.'

'Of course they won't,' I say, firmly.

'They will,' she says quietly. 'Because you're frightened of them.'

CHAPTER EIGHT

The first months of my pregnancy went so well and I never experienced the crippling morning sickness that had blighted the first trimester of my pregnancy with Stephanie. I'd almost convinced myself I was carrying a boy because the pregnancies were so different. Although secretly I wanted to have a brother for Stephanie and a son for George, I never voiced this because we had no way of knowing. I'd have hated for anyone to think that another daughter wasn't wanted.

When I miscarried at twelve weeks I was in total shock; there was no indication that anything was amiss and I'd felt so well that I'd assumed everything was fine. I thought that losing the baby was the very worst thing that could ever happen to me.

The day had started just like any other. Stephanie and I had been to a mother and toddler group at the church in the morning and she'd enjoyed playing on the trikes and ride- a-long toys while I'd chatted with two of the other mums that I'd made friends with. I remember that it was a lovely sunny day and as I'd pushed Stephanie home in the pushchair, I'd taken my coat off and slung it in the shopping basket underneath the pushchair so I could enjoy the April sunshine.

After we got home and had lunch, I'd put Stephanie up in her cot for a nap as was my usual routine and I was looking forward to having a sit down with an uninterrupted cup of tea and a look at the newspaper.

I'd made the tea and was walking into the lounge with the cup in my hand when the first pain hit me; it was so excruciating that I doubled over and the tea went flying all over the floor. I knew straight away that something was terribly wrong; pains like that weren't normal and all I could think was that I needed to get help. I crawled out to the hallway to get to the phone and managed to dial Mum's number.

The next time I knew anything was when I woke up in hospital; I have no recollection of anything after dialling Mum's number although obviously I did speak to her but I have no memory of it. How fortunate for me that I'd managed to ring her because the pain I was suffering was from an ectopic pregnancy. If the emergency services hadn't got to me quickly I'd most likely have died.

I was lucky to be alive.

I didn't feel lucky; the emergency surgery to save my life had involved removing a fallopian tube and I was told it was unlikely that I'd ever be able to get pregnant again. Not impossible, but unlikely. My dreams of a big family vanished in the space of one day that had started out like any other.

I returned home and although I tried to put a brave face on things I sank into a deep depression and just couldn't seem to pull myself together. I tried to tell myself that I still had Stephanie and that I should be grateful for that – and I was – but I couldn't shake the depression. Each morning when I woke I'd remember my loss and it was as much as I could do to get out of bed. I struggled to get through the days and felt as if I was walking through treacle. I truly thought that the ectopic pregnancy was the very worst thing that could ever happen to me.

How wrong I was.

CHAPTER NINE

When the doorbell rang on Monday evening at ten-past-seven I knew immediately there was only one person it could possibly be; Prue.

I took my time answering the door because I was determined I wasn't going to hurry to her command. I didn't put Rocky out in the garden either and I told Kayla to stay right where she was on the sofa. Kayla asked if I was sure that I didn't want her to go upstairs while I spoke to Prue but I said definitely not; this is her home and she has no need to hide away when I have visitors.

I did consider not answering the door at all but dismissed this idea because that would be avoiding Prue and the situation. I have no intention of doing that and she would only use that as proof of my inability to live my own life and make my own decisions. Although if Prue really annoys me I may use that tactic in future – because why should I tolerate someone I dislike in my own home?

Things are changing.

Kayla's remark last night that I'm afraid of Douglas and Prue made me do some serious thinking.

Am I afraid of them?

Quite honestly, I am. I think that I've become afraid of pretty much everything over the years, I'm afraid to make any impression in this world, afraid to express an opinion or show my feelings in case someone doesn't like it. I've spent so long trying not to upset other people that I've forgotten who I am.

I have allowed Douglas and Prue to exert their control over me to the point that I feel I have to seek permission to do what I want in my own home.

Well it stops right now; no more.

When the doorbell rings again, more insistently, I turn the hall light on and go to the front door and open it.

'Hello, Prue,' I say, with a big smile. 'What a lovely surprise.'

'Hello, Auntie Ria.' Prue stretches her mouth into her usual tight-lipped smile and I step back from the doorway to let her in.

'Come on through,' I say, closing the door and walking down the hallway to the lounge. Prue follows behind me and I can almost feel her disapproval in the air. We go into the lounge and Rocky trots up to us and proceeds to sniff Prue's legs. She stands frozen to the spot and looks at him with unconcealed disgust.

'You have a dog,' she states.

'Yes, I do,' I lie. I decide to go with her assumption that Rocky is mine as this will ensure that she cannot attempt to use him as leverage to push Kayla out.

'I didn't know you liked dogs,' she says accusingly, as Rocky takes one last sniff before losing interest in her. He trots over to Kayla and flops down onto the floor at her feet.

'You don't know a lot of things about me,' I retort, shocking myself and her.

'Oh.' She looks stunned by my answer. 'But you're allergic to dogs,' she insists.

'No, I'm not,' I say. 'It was George who was allergic and he's not here now, is he?'.

Prue stares at me and I stare back, determined not to be intimidated.

'Where on earth did you get it from?' she demands. 'It's huge; it'll eat you out of house and home and ruin the furniture. Whatever were you thinking of?'

'Him,' I say. 'It's a him and his name's Rocky. I got him from the dog's rescue centre.'

'What rescue centre? I didn't know we had one.' Prue narrows her eyes at me and I feel myself weakening, slightly. She would know too; no doubt when she *assists* old people into homes she gets rid of their pets for them. Probably straight to the nearest incinerator if I know her.

'Well, that just shows that you don't know

everything,' I retort, enjoying the look of annoyance on her face. 'Anyway.' I continue, after an awkward silence. 'Let me introduce you to Kayla, no doubt Douglas has told you all about her and she's the reason you're here.' The words come out bluntly and sound extremely rude but I find that I don't care. I just want to get this over with and for Prue to go away and leave us in peace.

Kayla stands up from the sofa and comes over and holds her hand out to Prue who looks down at it as if it's a wet fish.

'Hello, Prue, nice to meet you,' Kayla says. 'I've heard so much about you.'

And none of it good.

'Hello, Kylie, nice to meet you too.' Prue takes Kayla's hand and shakes it as briefly as possible.

'It's Kayla, not Kylie.' I say, flatly.

'Sorry, K-a-y-l-a,' Prue enunciates each letter carefully as if she were speaking a foreign language. I know she's doing it deliberately to undermine Kayla and I suddenly want to hit her and throw her out of my house. I cannot stand the woman yet I have to tolerate her coming to my home and poking her nose into my business as if she has a perfect right to.

Why? Why do I have to put up with her?

She's not even a relative of mine; she's a relative by marriage of George's, so why do I have anything to do with her? Is there a law that says I have to allow unpleasant people into my house to question my guests and my life? No, there isn't, and from now on she can be a bit nicer or next time I definitely won't answer the door to her.

Kayla goes and sits back down and Prue settles herself in the armchair opposite her.

So,' Prue says. 'I understand you're staying here under the college rent-a-room scheme, Kayla?'

Kayla opens her mouth to answer her but I butt in and answer for her. Rather rude of me but I feel that I need to put a stop to the interrogation before it starts.

'Yes she is,' I say. 'And it's working out very well.'

'And how is it that you're not living with your family?' Prue asks Kayla, completely ignoring me.

Kayla opens her mouth to speak but I flash a look at her and then walk over to Prue and stand directly in front of her to block her view of Kayla. I cross my arms, pull my shoulders back and give her the benefit of my full five-foot-two inches as I look down at her.

'Don't answer that, Kayla,' I say, while staring at Prue. 'It's none of Prue's business where you live and she's leaving now, aren't you Prue?'

The look on Prue's face is a picture and I can't think why I haven't done this before. My heart is racing and I'm glad that I have my arms crossed because I'm sure that my hands are shaking a little but I feel good, and I feel alive.

But most of all, I feel in control.

There's silence but Prue doesn't move an inch. I wonder if I'm going to have to forcibly eject her from my house.

I will if necessary.

Prue's shocked expression gradually fades and is replaced by a condescending smile.

'Really, Auntie Ria, I...' there's a Prue telling off coming, I can tell. I've heard it many times before but this time I stop her before she can get into full flight.

'You need to leave,' I say, talking over her. My voice sounds alien to me, calm and even and not at all how I feel. 'And you need to stop calling me auntie; I'm not your auntie and I never have been. Now I'd like you to go, please, before I say something I'll regret.'

Prue stares at me and I stare unflinchingly back, only the ticking of the clock on the mantelpiece breaking the silence.

'Okay,' Prue says, slowly. I move backwards and she stands up. 'I'll go but I'm going to speak to Douglas about this. I'm not sure you're thinking straight.'

Without another word she marches out into the hallway and I hear the front door open and close and that's it; she's gone.

❋ ❋ ❋

Kayla has made the decision not to go back to college for the last week before Christmas. She says that the place is in wind-down mode now and no work gets done as half of the students don't turn up because the lessons are mostly 'handouts' and 'old stuff'. I'm not quite sure what this means as it's a very long time since I was in any sort of education so I'm not in a position to argue. It's her life and I can hardly tell her what to do.

Kayla asked me why I didn't have a Christmas tree up. I told her that I haven't put a tree up for many years because it doesn't seem worth the effort of putting it all up just to have to take it all down again a few weeks later. She looked shocked and I can't say I blame her; as I was uttering the words I thought how completely miserable I sounded. I later realised that those words were exactly what George used to say and I was simply copying him.

Christmas is just another day to me but does it have to be that way? What if I actually made an effort, would that be so very bad? No, it wouldn't, I decided, so I asked Kayla if she'd go with me to buy a tree and some decorations and here we are, the tree is up and Kayla is adding the finishing touches to it.

We bought a real one which was Kayla's idea and not mine. I was ready to go and get a fake one but Kayla said no, we need a real one that *smells* like Christmas so we drove out to a place just outside of town where Kayla and her mum always get theirs from. Kayla negotiated a price with the man and he did a bit of hammering and cutting to the bottom of the tree to make a stand and then he shoved it into my car. We had to put the back seats down to get it in and we drove home very slowly with the boot lid open as the end of the tree was sticking out of the car. All the way home I was wondering how we were going to get it into the house because even though the Christmas tree man handled it as though it were nothing, I think Kayla and I would have trouble carrying it between us.

As I pulled the car up onto the drive Derek appeared from his back garden and watched as Kayla and I got out of the car. He plodded towards us and the closer he got the more nervous I became. I was just about to start panicking when, without a word, Derek pulled the tree out of the boot as if it weighed nothing and asked us where we wanted it. Kayla took charge and before we knew it the tree was installed in front of the lounge window between the sideboard and the television. Kayla says that we'll be able to see the lights twinkling from outside and it'll look festive and welcoming.

After he'd gone to the trouble of setting the tree up, I felt if only fair to offer Derek a cup of tea and a slice of Christmas cake for his efforts. He said yes but I think he felt very awkward; he sat on the edge of the sofa and drank the tea in two gulps and the cake in two bites and then got up, grunted *bye* and went back next door. I then sat and watched Kayla arrange the decorations on the tree; she's made a far better job of it than I ever did.

'Ta-da!' Kayla stands to the side of the tree and holds her arms out towards it.

'It looks fabulous, Kayla, you have a real flair for it,' I say. She does, too. All of the decorations are new; I'm sure there are some old ones in the loft but I decided that they could stay there because I want no memories of past Christmases.

We bought some large, shiny, red and silver baubles and red and silver ribbon which Kayla has somehow twirled into fabulous bows. The multicoloured lights twinkle and even Rocky seems mesmerised by them.

'Feels proper Christmassy now.' Kayla beams.

'It does,' I agree. I hold out the box of chocolate biscuits to her. 'Have another, it'll keep you going until dinner time.'

'I'm going to be a proper fatty,' she says, with a smile as she takes one.

Christmas carols are playing on the radio and as I watch Kayla bite into her biscuit, for the first time in forever, I feel a moment of true happiness.

The shrill of the doorbell shatters the ambience and in that moment I decide that the bell must go; I've always hated the sound of it. It's loud enough to wake the dead and I always feel that bad news is on the way when it rings.

'Who's that?' Kayla looks alarmed.

'Probably carol singers,' I say, soothingly as I get up and go out into the hallway. I don't think it's carol singers at all; if Prue has run true to form I know who it'll be.

I pull open the front door to be confronted by a middle-aged woman in a pale pink padded coat muffled up around the neck with a huge black scarf. She's carrying a briefcase and I know what she is before she even opens her mouth.

'Mrs Ria Simmonds?' she says, her voice muffled through the layers of scarf.

'Yes?'

'I'm Clara Newson from Social Services, I wonder if I might come in?'

CHAPTER TEN

Clara is seated on the sofa, cup of tea in one hand and Christmas biscuit in the other. She's removed the huge padded coat and scarf to reveal a knitted dress in chunky purple wool that looks very much like a blanket.

It's warm and cosy in the lounge and feels very festive and I'm pleased that her first impression of my home is a welcoming one. I'm hopeful that this will go some way to her agreeing to Kayla remaining here.

'So Kayla,' she asks through a mouthful of biscuit. 'When were you going to tell us where you were staying? You're supposed to keep in touch with us. Your mother's been frantic with worry as we had no idea where you were.'

Kayla makes a snorting sound and I wonder at the transformation in her since the social worker arrived. She's sitting hunched up on the floor against the wall next to the tree with her knees pulled up and her arms wrapped around her jean clad legs. The expression on her face is one that I haven't seen before and can only be described at mulish. She appears every inch the stroppy teenager now.

'Now come on, there's no need to be like that. It's not a lot to ask for you to let us know where you're living,' Clara continues. 'You may have fallen out with your mother but there's no need to cause her unnecessary worry.'

'Didn't need to let you or her know, did I?' Kayla says. 'Seeing as some big mouth's already told you.'

'I assume it was Prue that told you?' I look pointedly at Clara.

'It was,' she answers, completely unfazed. 'She mentioned something about the rent-a-room scheme but I think maybe she got her wires crossed because I checked and I couldn't find anything on the records. It would have been more straightforward had Kayla told me herself but we are where we are and we'll have to proceed from here.'

'I'm not going anywhere else and you can't make me.' Kayla rests her chin on her knees and glares at Clara.

'I'm sure here will be just fine,' Clara says calmly. 'Once I've conducted a risk assessment we can put things on a more formal basis.'

'Risk assessment?' I echo.

'Yes. Just a few details to complete.' She puts her cup of tea down on the arm of the chair, picks up her briefcase from the floor and snaps it open. She pulls out a large pad of paper and a pen.

She's going to ask me how Kayla and I met and I try desperately to think something that doesn't involve me finding her sitting on the edge of a six-storey drop in a car park and thinking she's going to commit suicide.

'So, how do you know each other?' Clara asks, as she studies the tin of biscuits before selecting a chocolate digestive.

I open my mouth with no idea of what I'm going to say and close it again when Kayla speaks.

'Ches Davies' mum and dad are Ria's next door neighbours,' Kayla says.

'Eileen from the homeless shelter?' Clara asks, taking a slurp of tea.

'Yeah,' Kayla says, sullenly.

'Okay, I see, I knew they'd moved but didn't realise it was next door.' Carla puts her teacup down and writes on the pad. I watch her, astounded that living next door to Eileen and Derek seems to be a good enough reason for Kayla to come and live with me.

'So.' She looks at me expectantly, pen poised over the paper. 'I'm going to need the names of all the people who are resident in this house.'

'Just me,' I say,

'No one else who stays on a regular basis?' she asks.

'No.'

She bends her head and scribbles on the pad; far more writing than is necessary to write *no*.

'So.' She looks up at me. 'If I could have your full name, age and employment details please.'

I give her my details and she writes them on her pad. I try to see what else she's written but it's a blur without my reading glasses.

'Visitors.' She looks up at me again. 'I need the names and addresses of all regular visitors to the house.'

'You've already met one of them and the other is her husband, Douglas.'

'Prue and Doug?'

I nod.

She writes some more; she must know them both well as she doesn't ask for their details. It seems strange to hear Douglas referred to as *Doug* by a perfect stranger; they obviously have a life and friends that I know nothing about.

'Okay, who else?' Clara looks at me expectantly, pen poised.

'No one,' I say. 'No one at all.'

❈ ❈ ❈

There's a distinctive smell to hospitals; if I were to arrive at one with my eyes shut there is no doubt that I would know where I was. I couldn't tell you what the smell is but I would recognise it, I'm certain.

Kayla has no idea that I'm here; when I left the house I told her that I have a dentist's appointment this afternoon. She seemed surprised when I told her and then I realised that she probably assumed that all old people have false teeth and don't have any of their own teeth left.

I thought about not coming to my appointment because I really didn't want to but then fear got the better of me; not fear of the illness itself but fear of what might happen if I didn't turn up. Would my non-attendance send up a red flag resulting in my next of kin being contacted? Would Douglas and Prue be informed of my non arrival? Could events snowball and they'd discover why I've been attending the hospital?

I've tried to convince myself that I'm being melodramatic and that there is a code of ethics that doesn't allow the medical profession to share one's medical records but equally, the other part of me knows.

Different rules apply when you're old.

Could I be forced to accept treatment that I don't want? If somehow Douglas and Prue were to find out what was wrong with me could they insist that I have the treatment even though I don't want it? Could they use my non-compliance as proof of me losing my faculties and force me to go into a home and give up my independence? Would giving a home to a young girl be used as evidence of my mind failing?

I fear that it could. My next door neighbour Nancy had all of her decisions made for her once she started showing signs of dementia. In no time at all her life wasn't her own and every decision was being made for her by other people.

It began with carers turning up at her door every day; they would fly inside in a hurry and scuttle out twenty minutes later. Three times a day they came, once in the morning to help her with her breakfast and to get dressed, at lunchtime to help her with getting her lunch and in the evening to put her to bed.

Sometimes the evening ones came very early at six o'clock; did that mean that she was put to bed early like a child? I rather think it did. The carers changed frequently so it was no wonder Nancy was confused with all of the different faces. There were male carers too, on occasion. I knew that Nancy would have hated this and to my shame I never said a word to her son; not one word. I should have said something even though it probably wouldn't have made any difference. It wasn't long before Nancy started refusing to let the carers in. A key safe was installed inside the porch so the carers could let themselves in but although Nancy had dementia she got wise to it. She began to push furniture up against the front door to stop them from opening the door.

I don't think the carers tried very hard once she started that as they were on a tight schedule and had to get to their next client. They didn't have the time to spend on someone who didn't want their help.

By this time her son was at his wits' end trying to hold down a stressful job and look after his mother, so Nancy was taken into a nursing home where twenty-four-hour care could be provided and he could have peace of mind knowing that she was safe. He was only trying to do what was best for her and truthfully, what else could he have done?

Nancy might have had dementia but a part of her knew what was happening; when the day came for her to go into the home, her son and a man I assume was from the nursing home had to drag her bodily out of her house, kicking and screaming. I couldn't bear to watch and stayed indoors. Nancy no longer knew who I was and I'd have been no help to her son but I still felt like a traitor and a coward.

And even though I was inside my house I could still hear her screams.

I visited Nancy several weeks after she moved into the nursing home and she had no idea who I was and thought I was one of her teachers from her childhood. She kept calling me *miss* and was cuddling a stuffed toy dog as if it were real. I wanted to cry for her. Her once perfectly coiffed hair was wild and straggly and she was barely recognisable. She'd been bathed and her hair was clean but she looked disturbed, deranged, even. Her clothes didn't look like hers and I wondered if what I'd heard about nursing homes was true; that all of the resident's clothing went into the laundry and once washed became a communal wardrobe. She wasn't my old friend Nancy anymore; she was a stranger to me and I to her.

I never went back.

Of course Nancy couldn't have stayed in her home; she could no longer look after herself and she wouldn't accept help so her son had no choice. There's nothing more he could have done but I was glad it wasn't me and I prayed that dementia wasn't to be my fate, too.

I push through the double doors from the corridor and approach the desk and give the receptionist my name. She taps efficiently on her keyboard and looks at her screen and points me towards the line of seats in the waiting area. I walk across and sit down; there are twelve seats in this alcove and besides myself there are four other people here. They're either looking at magazines or studying their feet, none of them make eye contact with me and I'm sure there'll be no idle chit chat about the weather here. A middle-aged woman in the seat opposite me looks up from her magazine and I inadvertently catch her eye. I smile at her but she stares at me blankly before dipping her head and resuming her reading. I'm certain she's not reading at all; she'll be thinking of what's to come and what her chances of survival are.

Unlike me who knows exactly how it's going to end.

I may have drifted through the last forty-three years like a sleep walker but I have no intention of continuing in that way. From now on, my life is my own. Today's appointment is to confirm to the consultant that I have no wish to go ahead with the first course of treatment – the treatment that will not cure me as the cancer is far too advanced but would, the consultant assured me, buy me some more time. He never specified how much time but from his eagerness to begin treatment immediately, I'm guessing it would be months and not years.

I'm going to tell them, again, that I don't wish to have treatment and want to enjoy what time I have left. I said this on my last appointment but the consultant insisted that I go away and think about it and discuss my options with my family before making a decision. I haven't changed my mind; nor have I discussed it with anyone.

Luckily, I feel well for most of the time but I know that I've been fortunate so far and that it won't last. According to the consultant, it won't be too long before I start to feel ill and today a care plan will be drawn up for when that occurs.

A blue uniformed nurse comes into the waiting area and calls my name.

'Maria Simmonds?'

I stand up and she smiles and asks me to follow her.

As I follow her down the corridor to the consultant's room I console myself with one simple fact.

This will be my last visit here.

CHAPTER ELEVEN

I struggled to cope after the miscarriage and I knew that George was slowly becoming exasperated with me. He kept telling me that we had a beautiful daughter and were very lucky. Some people, he reminded me, couldn't have children at all.

I knew he was right and I agreed with him completely but despite that I just couldn't seem to pull myself together. I had no energy at all and I found every day hard going. I'd even lost the joy in looking after Stephanie. Eventually Mum persuaded me that perhaps I needed some help so I made an appointment to see my GP to placate her although I couldn't see how a doctor could possibly help.

When I arrived for my appointment, as soon as I got into the doctor's room I burst into tears. He listened as I sat there and sobbed and then wrote me a prescription for Valium and told me to get plenty of rest. As I left the surgery I stuffed the prescription into my bag and decided that the visit had been a complete waste of time; there is no cure for a broken heart and never will be.

Nowadays, of course, there would be counselling or an opportunity to talk to others who had suffered a similar loss but then there was nothing; just the assumption that the miscarriage had happened because there was something wrong with the baby. Better to have a miscarriage, seemed to be the thinking, than have a baby with a defect.

I carried that prescription around in my handbag for over a week before I took it to the chemist to have it filled. I have always had an aversion to taking medicine of any sort; I didn't even like taking the iron tablets that the hospital had given me when I was pregnant.

It was George who forced the issue. Of course he never told me I had to take the tablets but I knew he was losing patience with me. I'd catch him looking at me with a frown or he'd sigh at the state of the house when he came home from work. I felt compelled to do something to get our lives back to normal and although I had no faith that the tablets would help, they couldn't do any harm.

It was a difficult time for George without the trauma of the miscarriage, he was having a particularly stressful time at work as he'd just been promoted and had to prove his worth. He didn't actually say the words and tell me to pull myself together, but I knew he was thinking it. I didn't blame him; he was used to coming home from work to a peaceful environment and a home cooked evening meal, not a shambles of a house and a constantly crying wife.

Mum and Dad helped all they could and I knew I

was being selfish but I couldn't seem to shake myself out of it. George had lost a baby too, I kept reminding myself, but it didn't help me because I felt incapable of getting myself back to normal.

George's mother came round several times and helped me with Stephanie but I knew that I annoyed her. She never said it out loud but it was obvious by the pursed lips and the whispered conversations with George that she thought I was wallowing in self pity. She'd had several miscarriages herself before she had George and I knew that she thought I was making a meal of things.

So I went to the chemist and got the prescription filled but I still stopped short of taking them, I hoped that somehow, magically, I'd start to feel better without them.

I didn't, of course, so after another awful week had gone by I forced myself to take the Valium because I realised that I wasn't going to get better on my own. I soon found that the tablets didn't make me feel better but dulled my emotions and although I didn't feel any happier, I wasn't continually crying. As the weeks went on I began to feel more and more zombie-like and all I wanted to do was sleep.

After a couple of months I decided that I had to stop taking the tablets because the emotional pain was preferable to the numbness. But I couldn't; I didn't have the strength to make myself stop. I now know that I was addicted to the valium but I didn't know that at the time; I just thought that I was weak and selfish.

George was barely speaking to me by this time and seemed to think that my misery was a choice. Every night when I went to bed I'd promise myself that tomorrow morning I'd throw the tablets into the bin and pull myself together and be a proper wife and mother.

But when I woke in the morning it was as much as I could do to get out of bed.

I felt as if my whole life was falling apart and I could do nothing to stop it.

And then the very worst thing in the world happened.

CHAPTER TWELVE

We're out on the heath and Rocky is bounding around as if he's been released from prison. Kayla and I are wrapped up warm against the cold in hats, scarves and gloves and our breath blows plumes of cold in front of us as we march along.

It's still bitterly cold and there's a definite pink tinge to the sky. When I see the sky that colour I call it a snow sky because it has that strange hue that I've seen before when snow is just around the corner. I know that the wind had changed direction too from the weather vane in my garden; it's swung around from north and is now pointing firmly to the east; a sign surely, of wintry weather to come. I say as much to Kayla.

'That'd be well cute,' she says, throwing Rocky's ball into the scrubby grass. 'A proper white Christmas.'

'It would be nice,' I agree, as I watch Rocky lollop in an ungainly fashion after the ball. 'Instead of the usual warm rain.'

As we crunch along the stony, rough path in our sturdy boots, it takes me a moment to recognise the stocky figure loitering under a tree ahead of us.

'Alright, Ches,' Kayla calls out with a wave as we draw closer to him.

Chester, my next door neighbour's son, flushes deep scarlet and grunts *hiya*. He pulls his hoodie down further over his head and shoves his hands into his trouser pockets. He must be freezing in the flimsy top.

'Alright?' he mutters.

It takes me a moment to realise that he's talking to me; he's never acknowledged me before when I've seen him in the street and I'd stopped bothering to speak to him after several attempts as he never replied. I hide my surprise and say *hello*.

'Where you been?' he asks Kayla as he saunters over to us. 'Haven't seen you at college for ages.'

'I've had a few weeks off,' Kayla says breezily. 'Family stuff to do, you know? I'll be back after Christmas.'

'You ain't missed much.' Chester falls into step next to Kayla. 'It's just the same as school, no one does anything before the holidays. None of the teachers can be arsed. All they want to do is give handouts out and go to meetings.'

'That's what I thought, I can do more work at

home on my own. Me and my nan have just been chilling and getting ready for Crimbo,' Kayla says.

I can't help the warm glow I feel when Kayla refers to me as her nan; it makes me feel wanted and as if I belong instead of being in my usual position on the outskirts of life. I could have had a granddaughter of Kayla's age if things had been different.

'Yeah, Mum's been well busy, too,' Chester says. 'Getting all the food in for the shelter, y'know? She moans about it every year but I know it's what keeps her going. She wouldn't do it if she didn't love it.'

Kayla laughs and her and Chester chat as I amble along beside them. I don't feel excluded although they're not including me in the conversation. I feel comfortable and at ease, which is an unusual feeling for me.

We reach the park exit and Kayla calls Rocky over but he ignores her and continues to sniff every blade of grass. After repeated attempts she resorts to pulling a biscuit out of her pocket to bribe him. He bounds over and she clips his lead onto his collar while he inhales the biscuit.

As we head towards the exit I see another hooded teenager at the park gates and realise that it's one of Chester's friends who I've seen in the street before. Chester strides off towards him, calling out *see ya Kayla's nan* to me as he goes. I chuckle as he struts towards his friend; I'm sure his wide legged stride and the strip of under-pant waistband that he's showing is for Kayla's benefit. Judging by his bright scarlet face when he saw her, I think he has a crush on her.

'I think Ches has a soft spot for you, Kayla,' I say, when he's out of earshot.

'What? No way. We're just mates,' she says. 'I don't want a boyfriend, thanks.'

'I think he was hanging around waiting for you back there.'

'No, he just likes to chat,' she insists. 'I know him from my old school, he used to be in my class.'

'Oh, I didn't realise.'

'Yeah, we were in the same class right from year three. I always used to feel a bit sorry for him because he got bullied about his weight a lot, being, you know, a bit on the big side. They might spout all this 'be kind' stuff but some kids don't take any notice of it. It didn't help that he used to rise to it; I think he spent most of his time crying. I don't really know his mum and dad but they do a lot for the homeless shelter because Ches helps sometimes and he used to get bullied for that, as well.'

I look at her in shock.

'Do they? Does he?'

'Yeah,' Kayla says. 'Ches's mum works at the homeless shelter and the whole family give up their Christmas day to cook Christmas dinner and help out there. His dad does the picks-up for the charity bags, you know, the ones people put their old stuff in. Which is funny, really, because they haven't got much themselves.'

I try to take in what Kayla's just told me. My rough and ready neighbours who I've decided, don't *fit in,* are not the people that I thought they were. I've judged them totally on what they look like and the fact that Derek is careless about where he plants his feet.

'Ches told me that they moved here to get away from their old neighbours 'cos they were so vile. They lived next door to the roughest family on the estate and they made life unbearable for them; his mum nearly had a nervous breakdown. People can be horrible, can't they?'

'They can indeed,' I say.

❉ ❉ ❉

We're half-way home when it starts to snow; it begins with little flakes floating playfully in the air but by the time we're nearly home they've turned into huge flakes that feel blizzard-like. The windscreen wipers sweep furiously from side to side and I'm thankful that we've not far to go. I never used to drive in the snow on the rare occasion that we had it; George always did the driving and if we had a few days of it we'd batten down the hatches and not leave the house.

Like two old people.

When I was young I used to love it when it snowed; the creaking sound that my boots made when I walked on freshly fallen snow and the strange stillness of a new white world. Everything looked and sounded different when it had snowed heavily.

When did that change, I wonder? When did I get so old that I stopped noticing everything around me? I know when it was and there was a good reason for it but did I really have to stay like that, did I really have to spend the last forty-odd years living in name only?

I know the answer to that question, too, but it's not the reason that I thought it was for so many years.

The pink-tinged sky has changed to a dark grey and it feels as if the sky has lowered itself although I know that's not possible and is only an illusion. In the ten minutes that we've been in the car the light is already starting to fade and I'm glad that we didn't stay any longer at the heath.

I asked Kayla to look out for Chester as we pulled out of the car park so we could give him and his friend a lift. Chester's thin hoodie would offer little protection against the biting wind but we didn't see them; maybe they took a short cut. I find myself hoping that Chester gets home okay and isn't too cold.

I asked Kayla some more about her college course on the way and although she tried to hide her enthusiasm she couldn't help but let her absolute love of art show through. I've told her again that she must use the paints and art equipment that George left in the bedroom; I said that if she doesn't I'm just going to throw it all out anyway.

I've made her promise to use it and show me some of her work. I have no knowledge of what is good art or not but I know what I like.

As we turn into my street there's already a covering of snow on the ground and it's getting thicker by the minute. I pull up onto the drive and turn the engine off with relief. As I look at the house I'm surprised to see a woman trying unsuccessfully to shelter from the blizzard under the small canopy over my front door. She's small and round and is bundled up in a bright yellow puffer jacket with a huge bobble hat pulled down over unruly curly hair that refuses to be covered.

'Oh,' I say, opening the car door. 'I wonder who that is?'

Kayla doesn't answer and makes no move to get out of the car.

'Kayla?'

'It's my mum,' she says, with a grim look on her face.

'Oh, I see,' I say.

'No,' Kayla says quietly. 'You don't.'

CHAPTER THIRTEEN

Kayla was all for not letting her mum into the house.

I was rather shocked at her reaction to the sight of her mother and for the second time in as many days I witnessed her Jekyll and Hyde transformation from amenable young women into belligerent teenager.

I insisted on Deanna – I had to ask her to introduce herself as Kayla flatly refused – coming into the house. We went through to the lounge and I put the fire on straight away and turned the Christmas tree lights on to make it cosier and then left them to it to go and make a cup of tea. I took Deanna's coat into the kitchen and hung it on the chair next to the radiator to dry and then towelled Rocky down with one of my best towels – I have hundreds so why not use them – and put the kettle on.

I took my time and laid out a tray with a plate of biscuits and cut some slices of Christmas cake and put them on a plate too. I wanted to give them time to talk without me listening in. When the kettle boiled I still made no move to go into the lounge because I could hear the faintest murmur of voices, although I couldn't hear what they were saying.

I sat at the kitchen table stroking Rocky's ears and I couldn't help feeling sad. Kayla has only been staying with me for a short while but I've grown to like her very much; she's good company and I've felt real happiness for the first time in many years. I know that I don't deserve that happiness but the selfish part of me has enjoyed it anyway. We don't always get what we deserve, do we?

The thought of Kayla leaving and me going back to being on my own again is almost unbearable. I realise that my silly daydreams where I'm her nan and she's happy to stay here are just that – silly dreams. The reality is that she'll make up with her mum – which is only right and proper – and go back home. She has her proper family and I'm not part of it and never will be, no matter how much I might wish that I was.

The thought of a miserable Christmas with Prue and Douglas is almost more than I can bear. I've been given a glimpse of how life should be and it's made my solitary, miserable existence seem even worse.

I could bring my plan forward to escape but I'm loath to do so as the arrangements are made and it'll be complicated to change them. I'm sure that once I'm away from here, I can go through with it but in this house I don't think that I'm brave enough. Also, if I don't do it properly and make a mess of it, the consequences are unthinkable.

I take a deep breath and get up from the chair and flick the kettle to boil again as the water is now only lukewarm. I can get through Christmas and New Year, I tell myself. We're only talking of a couple of weeks and what's a couple of weeks compared to the last forty odd years? A mere drop in the ocean.

I can do it.

Kayla and her mum will make up and that's a good thing; I'm pleased for them both because I'm not completely selfish.

The kettle comes to the boil and I pour the water into the teapot, I give it a good stir and replace the lid. I tilt my head and listen for a moment; the murmurings from the lounge seem to have stopped. I carefully pick up the tray and carry it carefully into the hallway, place it on the hall table, open the lounge door and then pick it up and take it in.

❊ ❊ ❊

'I'm not coming home and you can't make me.' Kayla is sitting on the sofa, arms crossed, with

Rocky sitting at her feet. This is the third time she's uttered the words and I can't help but feel a little sorry for Deanna.

Despite Kayla telling me that her mother threw her out of the house, it's not seeming like that's quite what happened from what Deanna's been saying. Softly spoken and looking like a plumper version of Kayla, she's insisted that she never threw Kayla out but rather than Kayla left of her own accord.

'Kayla,' Deanna says. 'I just want things to be how they used to be and for you to come home, we were happy, weren't we? Didn't we always used to have fun?'

'Should of thought of that before you moved *him* in,' Kayla says, sticking out her bottom lip and scowling.

Deanna sighs and I detect the merest hint of exasperation.

'Okay, I can see we're getting nowhere. I'm sorry.' She stands up and looks down at Kayla. 'But I can only say sorry so many times and actually Kayla, I *never* threw you out so stop saying it. You know that I would *never* do that so please stop telling everyone that I did. I made a mistake with Russ and I admit that but I *never* put him before you. I did *believe* you but I was in shock and you never gave me a chance to tell you that because you stormed out. I had no idea where you'd gone and I was frantic with worry. If that social worker hadn't contacted me to let me know where you were I'd still be in the dark. I was shocked that you could do that, I thought I brought you up better than that.'

Kayla colours slightly and lowers her eyes.

'When Russ came home from work that night his bags were packed and waiting for him outside the front door,' Deanna continues. 'I was more than ready to make a complaint to the police about him with you but you never even gave me a chance.'

'The police?' Kayla stammers.

'Yes, the police. Grown men shouldn't be perving on under-age girls and I want to make sure he never does it again. He's not the man I thought he was.'

'I don't want to go to the police,' Kayla says, quietly.

'He shouldn't be allowed to get away with it,' Deanna says.

'I know, but he didn't actually *do* anything, I didn't let him.'

'Thank God for that,' Deanna says. 'But that doesn't change the fact that he tried. He needs to be stopped from doing it again.'

'I can't face all the questioning so don't try and guilt trip me into it just to make yourself feel better,' Kayla mutters.

Deanna sighs and rolls her eyes.

'For God's sake, Kayla, stop twisting everything I say,' she says. 'I'm really trying here but you have to help me a bit. I just want things to be like they were before and put all this behind us. You need to come home.' She smiles. 'Because how am I going to do Christmas without you? You know I'm rubbish at putting the tree up and making the decorations.'

Kayla relaxes her arms and I see her glance at our tree, and I sense that she's relenting, that if Deanna carries on she'll give in and go home.

Deanna deserves to be forgiven; she's a good mother, Kayla admitted this to me herself. She made the silly mistake of picking the wrong boyfriend, of trusting the wrong man; a mistake that anyone could make. It wasn't deliberate; she was let down by him as much as Kayla. They should put this episode behind them and Kayla should go home, back to where she belongs.

I know all of this and yet I can't lose her and go back to being on my own, not yet. Just a bit longer, the selfish part of me demands, just a little longer.

'Why don't you come for Christmas here?' I suddenly blurt out to Deanna. She looks at me in shock and opens her mouth to speak but I carry on speaking, aware that I'm gabbling. If I keep talking then there's less chance for her to say no; less chance that I'll have to spend Christmas alone, or worse than that, with Douglas and Prue

'Let Kayla stay here until after Christmas while she sorts herself out and you come here for Christmas as well. I've plenty of room, you can stay over for the whole Christmas weekend.'

I feel my face flush and I bite my lip; I've embarrassed them both and myself as well. I sounded

desperate.
   I am desperate.

CHAPTER FOURTEEN

I wanted to die; anything to stop the pain of losing my darling Stephanie.

I can hardly bear to think of the days and weeks after she'd gone; even forty-three years later the pain hasn't diminished, it's there all of the time underneath the surface; an anecdote to my every action.

I've thought of suicide many times, at first every breath that I drew I yearned to be my last. Only the guilt stopped me from killing myself; how could I do that to George? How could I leave him alone to bear his grief? Hadn't he already suffered enough? I knew that I had no choice but to carry on living but each night I prayed that I'd die in my sleep and never wake up.

Because then I wouldn't have to endure the heartbreak of waking each morning to those first few seconds of blissful normality before I remembered; before the truth hit me with the force of a speeding train.

It was my fault that Stephanie was dead; I'd killed her.

If I'd pulled myself together it would never have

happened; if I'd been a proper wife and mother Stephanie would still be alive. If I'd stopped wallowing in self-pity and been grateful for what I had, Stephanie would still be here.

I had only myself to blame and even though George never uttered one word of blame to me I knew that I was guilty. He never blamed me, not once, even though I deserved it. We were still young and I him to leave me and start anew; he was young enough to have a new life with a new family. He was horrified and said that he would never leave me; that we would have a different kind of life but it could still be a good life once we'd got over our loss. His words shocked me as much as mine had shocked him because I knew that I would never get over the loss of my little girl.

I know that our friends and family thought I was to blame, but of course they never said this to me because hadn't I suffered enough? There was no doubt that I would blame myself for the rest of my life and that was surely punishment enough.

If only; two small words that meant so much.

If only I hadn't been so weak-willed and selfish, if only I'd looked after Stephanie properly, if only I'd never gone to the doctors, if only I'd never got the tablets. The list was endless and I actually thought I might go insane with the what ifs that were running on a loop through my mind.

I knew that those tablets were poisonous to children, I knew. I thought I'd been so careful to always put them out of reach so that Stephanie couldn't get to them; not just those tablets but any and all medi-

cines. I kept them high up on the book shelf in the lounge where there was absolutely no possibility that she would be able to reach them. The house might be a mess, I told myself, but I still looked after Stephanie properly and put her needs first. I might have lost all pride in a home that was once spotless but I could still look after my child. What did it matter if the lounge was a shambles of discarded toys, empty coffee cups and baskets of washing? Caring for Stephanie was important and nothing else.

Except that my carelessness meant that the tablets weren't on the shelf and I wasn't as careful as I thought I was In the stupor that had become my new normality, I had left the tablets lying around where Stephanie could find them. But by the time we'd realised that the tablets were causing Stephanie's illness it was far, far too late.

Nothing could be done to save her.

And so began my life sentence; I'd killed my own child.

CHAPTER FIFTEEN

My tickets arrived this morning; pretty good going considering the Christmas post is in full swing. The girl in the travel agents wanted me to go in and collect them as she was nervous of entrusting them to the Post Office so close to Christmas but I assured her it would be fine. I promised her that if I hadn't received them by the thirtieth of December I'd go into their office so she could print me off a new set. I won't need to bother now but I think I'll still pop in and thank her for all of her help once I've been to the solicitors to finalise things next week. I'll take some Christmas chocolates in as a little thank you gift.

It's strange to think that in fifteen days time I'll be boarding a ship in Southampton and setting off on a world cruise; the cruise that George always told me that we couldn't afford. I used to wonder if a world cruise could put miles between me and my memories. It was also something that George and I could have done as a couple instead of the usual holidays in a plush golf resort with all of his golfing cronies and their wives. I found the effort of being sociable and making pointless small talk more and more exhausting as the years went by. George may have enjoyed the golf and the camaraderie of his friends but to me it was more of a strain than our normal day to day life.

I can't blame George too much; the prospect of three months stuck on a ship with only me for company was obviously too much for him to bear. I firmly believe that he should have started afresh with someone else after we lost Stephanie; he seemed to recover much more quickly from our loss and although on the surface I appeared quite normal; underneath the pain was unbearable. I put a smile on my face for his sake but I'd changed and I wasn't the person I used to be. I was quieter and more reserved, the fun-loving extrovert that he'd fallen in love with was gone forever.

But it doesn't matter now.

Now I need to look to my future.

Since George died I've mastered internet searching and using the computer and discovered that my keyboard skills as a former secretary have never left me. I spent a lot of time on George's computer researching cruise statistics before I made my plan – making sure to delete my search history afterwards of course – and they made for very interesting reading. Whilst no cruise line would give an exact number of deaths per year, one cruise line insider admitted that up to three people per week die on cruises worldwide, particularly on lines that typically carry older passengers. Although I couldn't find a definitive figure, it's also not uncommon for passengers to be lost overboard from cruise ships either. The combination of old age, alcohol and stormy weather are apparently just right for falling overboard and never being seen again.

It's amazing what you can learn from a computer, far easier than looking it up at the library. I should have got to grips with computers years ago and not let George put me off. Whenever I suggested that he teach me he'd say that I'd be bored. He said it wasn't necessary for me to learn as he managed all of the household finances and was happy to do so.

Another thing that doesn't matter now.

The only person who knows about my cruise is Kayla. She was thrilled for me and made me promise to take lots of photographs of the places that I visit and to Whatsapp them to her. I think it might have made her feel a bit better about moving back to her mum's too, after my desperate performance of practically begging them to stay for Christmas. I told her that it was something that I'd always wanted to do and that I had to do it before I got too old – an almost laughable comment to make to a seventeen-year-old who thinks that thirty is over the hill.

It'll be a surprise – or maybe a shock – when I announce it to Douglas and Prue this evening. They're coming for dinner tonight and Kayla and I are cooking it. Aside from the news about the cruise I'll also be telling them that I won't be going to their house for Christmas day this year as I'm staying at home with Kayla and Deanna.

Douglas and Prue are not invited.

They wouldn't want to come if I did ask them but I know that they would feel compelled to accept the invitation if I issued it. I want to avoid that because they'd only spoil the day. So as they're not invited for Christmas day, we're having a Christmas dinner of sorts this evening; roast chicken with all the trimmings and Christmas pudding and ice cream to follow. Kayla helpfully prepped all of the vegetables before hurrying off and shutting herself in her room. She's been doing that a lot for the past few days and has been keeping the door to her bedroom firmly closed. She says that all will be revealed in due course. I think she might be painting something but I haven't asked.

After my desperate invitation to Kayla's mother on Friday to stay for Christmas, there was an embarrassing silence in the room. I was about to apologise and retract the offer when Deanna said that it was very generous of me to ask and was I sure? I assured her that I was and Deanna looked meaningfully at Kayla. There was an uncomfortable silence before Kayla sullenly shrugged her shoulders and snapped 'Yeah, alright. STAY.'

Deanna beamed a big smile and got up and went over to Kayla and put her arms around her. Kayla sat immobile for a moment and then relented and hugged her mother back. I got up to go out to the kitchen to leave them alone to talk things through because I felt I was intruding. As I reached the door Kayla called out to me and I turned to see them both standing up looking at me.

'Thank you,' said Deanna.

'Yes, thank you,' Kayla agreed. 'Sorry I've been such a brat Ria, but I'm over it now and the three of us are going to have the best Christmas ever, aren't we Mum?'

'We are,' agreed Deanna. 'The very best.'

I looked at them and felt almost moved to tears at the kindness of them both. I then sat back down and poured the tea out to give myself a chance to compose myself and not seem more of an old fool than I already did.

They're very kind people and I don't deserve their kindness.

But I'm going to take it anyway.

* * *

Prue is pushing the roast potatoes around her plate as if hoping that the movement will somehow make them disappear into thin air. She's eaten the tiniest piece of chicken possible and most of the vegetables but little else. All of the fat and salt used in the cooking will be giving her an anxious time. I want to tell her to eat up and do herself a favour because she looks like she needs a good meal but I restrain myself; I'm determined to be nice to her tonight.

I put the last piece of potato into my mouth and lay my knife and fork neatly across my plate. I chew, swallow and take a sip of the wine that Kayla and I chose from Waitrose. Very nice if a little dry.

'I have an announcement to make,' I say.

Three pairs of eyes swivel towards me and I smile uncertainly. 'I'm going on a cruise after Christmas,' I say, with a smile.

'A cruise?' Prue's brows knit together and for a moment I wonder if she's going to tell me that I'm not allowed.

'Yes. A world cruise. Well,' I add, with a laugh. 'Not quite the whole world; twenty-three countries over one hundred and twenty-one days.'

'That's four months!' exclaims Prue.

'Yes, it is,' I agree. 'How fabulous is that?'

'But...' Prue looks at Douglas who's suddenly finding his empty plate extremely interesting. 'Are you going on your own?'

'Of course,' I snap, momentarily forgetting my promise to be nice to her.

'But do you think that's wise?' Prue looks at me intensely. 'That's a very long time to be away from home.'

'Well, that's the thing, Prue,' I say. 'If I want to see the world on a ship it does take a long time. The idea is that it'll be relaxing and it'll be a complete change from normal life.'

'Douglas?' Prue frowns and stares at him, ignoring what I've just said. 'What do you think about this? What have you got to say about it?'

Douglas shrugs and gives a sheepish smile.

'What's that supposed to mean?' she demands. 'You surely can't think it sensible for a woman of her age to go off gallivanting around the world alone?'

The silence stretches and just as it's about to become embarrassing, Douglas speaks.

'It's just a holiday, Prue,' Douglas says, surprising me.

Prue purses her lips and narrows her eyes at Douglas before turning to me. He's going to be in trouble when they get home.

'I'm sorry, but I don't think it's a good idea at all. To be quite honest with you, I've become rather concerned about your behaviour lately, what with the whole *inviting someone to live with you thing.*' She raises her eyebrows in Kayla's direction, who I can see is trying very hard not to laugh.

I say nothing but stand up and begin to collect the empty plates. I'm not surprised at her reaction; the only surprise is that Douglas isn't joining in with her.

'Auntie Ria,' Prue stands up and pulls herself up to her full height in an attempt to intimidate me and impress her authority on me. 'I think we need to discuss this matter properly in private. Just the three of us. You, me and Douglas.'

'It's not really up for discussion,' I say, in a casual manner as I stack the plates. 'And besides, it's all booked and I've ordered lots of new clothes from Marks and Spencer to take with me.'

'I'm sure if we explain the circumstances the cruise company will give you a refund,' she says, waving her hand dismissively as if swatting a fly. 'And there'll be no problem returning the clothes to Marks, they're always happy to give a refund.'

'The circumstances?' I ask.

'Well yes, because you've gone and booked a world cruise without talking it over with us, of course.'

'So you think that I'm not capable of booking a holiday on my own?' I ask.

Prue looks at me in shock. 'How could you say something like that? Of course we don't think that, it's just that we want what's best for you.'

'No you don't,' I say, quietly. 'You want to treat me as if I'm a child, not a grown woman with a mind of her own. The cruise is booked and it's not up for discussion with you or anyone else. I'm going whether you like it or not so why don't you just sit back down and do yourself a favour and actually eat something with some calories in it.'

Prue stares at me in shock whilst slowly lowering herself back down into the chair.

And maybe I'm imagining it, but out of the corner of my eye I'm sure that I can see the merest hint of a smile on Douglas's face.

I pick up the stack of plates and carefully carry them through to the kitchen and put them on the draining board. Once I've put the plates down I can see that my hands are shaking. I grip the edge of the draining board to steady them and stare out of the kitchen window at the back garden.

My reflection stares back at me from the window pane and I look at myself in surprise.

I'm smiling.

CHAPTER SIXTEEN

When George had his first heart attack he thought he was going to die, he really did. It was such a shock because there were no signs that he was even ill; he was fit and appeared as healthy as he always had and at first he thought he had indigestion. The mild indigestion quickly turned to excruciating pain and then I too, thought that he was going to die.

And that is the one and only reason that he confessed to me what he'd done.

He wanted to unburden himself before he met his maker.

He wanted my forgiveness.

As we waited for the ambulance he whispered that he had something he had to tell me and for a moment I thought he was going to tell me that he'd had an affair. I would have forgiven him that, I wouldn't even have blamed him very much because there have been times during the last forty odd years when I haven't been much of a wife to him. Although I have tried my best; I hid my grief well after the first few years because I thought George deserved to be happy, even though I wasn't. But still; if he'd had an affair I would have forgiven him because he forgave me for something far worse.

He hadn't had an affair; and when he actually told me what he'd done I was stunned. He begged my forgiveness and I told him that I forgave him because I couldn't really take in what he was telling me; I couldn't quite believe what he was telling me.

And, as it turned out, he didn't die, not then, he lived for another nine months. After he confessed we never talked of what he'd told me again because what would have been the point? It had been said and couldn't be taken back.

But I never did forgive him, although he didn't know that. I treated him in exactly the same way as I always had and he had no idea how I felt. I tried so hard, I really did, but I just didn't have it in me. All I could think about was that he'd let me destroy myself for all those years, that he'd let me blame myself for every single minute of every single day, over and over again.

Because it wasn't my fault that Stephanie died, it was his.

When he came home from work that last evening that Stephanie was alive, I was upstairs bathing her. He said that he walked into the lounge and looked at the mess and clutter everywhere and felt exasperated and angry and just wanted our life back how it used to be. He said he couldn't understand why I couldn't pull myself together like he had. As he was about to put his car keys on the bookcase shelf, the sight of the jumble of tissues and clutter on there so enraged him that he'd angrily swept it all off the shelf and onto the floor. Of course he didn't know then that my tablets were amongst the clutter.

But he realised later.

By the time I'd come back downstairs with Stephanie he'd calmed down and picked the clutter up from the floor and put everything back on the shelf.

But not the bottle of tablets; he'd missed them.

I never noticed they were missing; I took a tablet every evening before I bathed Stephanie and had already taken one so had no need to look for them. When I found several tablets scattered amongst the toys on the floor then next day it was already too late; there were no child proof bottle caps in those days and my clever girl had opened the bottle easily. The bottle had been pushed underneath the sofa and yes, if the lounge hadn't been such a mess I would have noticed sooner and Stephanie could have been saved.

I wasn't blameless.

But neither was George; if he hadn't swept everything onto the floor Stephanie would still be alive.

George knew that Stephanie's death was his fault too but he never spoke up; he let me blame myself for over forty years. I would have forgiven him if he'd told me at the time; I wouldn't have blamed him because no one is perfect and he was under such a lot of stress. The loss of Stephanie was punishment enough.

Yes, I definitely would have forgiven him.

Then.

So we never spoke of it again in those last nine

months before he died and outwardly our lives continued as normal. But inside, underneath, everything had changed. And I tried so hard not to but I couldn't stop myself.

I began to hate him.

CHAPTER SEVENTEEN

Incredibly, and the first time for many years, we're having a white Christmas. And not just a sprinkling, either. There's a proper, satisfying, thick layer of fresh snow outside and the world looks like a winter wonderland. Even the lamp posts look pretty.

Kayla, Deanna and I have decided we're going to open our presents after Christmas dinner. The gifts that I've wrapped are underneath the tree and I notice that some others have been added to them; I haven't looked closely but I assume that they're from Deanna to Kayla.

George and I never bothered with Christmas gifts and hadn't done for many years. We told ourselves that we had everything we needed and could buy whatever we wanted so what was the point of buying pointless gifts? We reasoned that it would just be buying for the sake of it and therefore a complete waste of money.

Although actually, now that I come to think about it, this was George's opinion and not mine, but as with everything else I just went along with what he wanted. It's not George's fault; I have a mind of my own so I have only myself to blame that everything in our life was done his way. I rarely objected to anything he said and if I did challenge him about anything I was easily talked around to his way of thinking.

I see quite clearly now that I should have got myself a job and made some sort of an independent life for myself instead of relying on George for everything. I lacked the impetus to do anything other than struggle through each day and I have wasted the last forty-odd years drifting along in a stupor.

Not that any of it matters now because it's all too late. I can't blame George for my own failings but if I'd known the truth about Stephanie's death perhaps things would have been different; perhaps I would have been different. I would have still blamed myself and carried the guilt with me but it wouldn't have been so unbearable because George and I could have helped each other through. I've asked myself if I wallowed in my grief and guilt and I know most people would say that I definitely had; perhaps I did. Many people have lost children and they don't allow it to ruin their entire life; they recover eventually. I didn't go around the whole of my life looking miserable because I *did* manage to put a brave face on things; several years after we lost Stephanie I managed to pull myself together – in other people's eyes anyway – and give the appearance of being normal, but inside I was dying. I've never spoken to anyone, other than George, about my grief so I don't know whether the way I felt inside was *normal*. I felt that I owed it to George to at least appear normal as he refused to leave me and no one would have guessed from my demeanour how I really felt. Eventually even George assumed that I was okay; as the years went by we talked less and less of her and those conversations were always instigated by me. I honestly think that George would have been happier never talking about her at all. He said that it just dragged everything up and what was the point of constantly going over it all? Perhaps he was right.

Our friends – or rather George's friends – had me down as the quiet, stay-at-home, reserved type and I know that 'the wives' couldn't understand how I'd managed to bag George for myself when he could have had his pick of women. Most of them didn't know the real me, you see, before it happened, when I was pretty and vivacious and the life and soul of the party.

So maybe I have wallowed and I should have pulled myself together years ago, I really don't know, but I do know that it's pointless to dwell on it any longer. For the first time in years I feel happy and I'm having a better Christmas than I ever dreamed possible. It's time to look to the future, short though that may be.

'This turkey is delicious,' Deanna says, spearing another slice onto her fork.

'It's lush,' Kayla agrees, chomping on a mouthful.

I have to agree; it *is* delicious and I can't help feeling a little proud. I've always been a good cook and I rather think that George took me for granted. I wonder how he would have fared if he'd had to suffer Prue's dry-roasted potatoes and vegetables so *al dente* that they're barely edible.

We tuck into our meals with gusto and when I finally place my knife and fork together on my empty plate, I'm delighted to see that Deanna and Kayla have already finished and have eaten every single scrap.

'Pudding?' I suggest, as I sit back in the chair. 'Or do we want a breather?'

Deanna blows her cheeks out and rolls her eyes.

'A breather, I think,' she says, with a smile.

'Me too,' Kayla says. 'I'm stuffed.'

I stand up ready to clear the table but Deanna stops me with a firm *I'll do it* so I sit back down and let her ferry the plates out to the kitchen. I hear the dishwasher door open and the rattle of the plates as she stacks them inside.

'Should we do our presents before pudding?' Kayla asks. '

'Whatever you like,' I say, with a smile. 'I really don't mind.'

'I think we should,' Kayla says. 'Because I'm not going to be able to fit any more food in for at least a couple of hours.'

'Nor me,' Deanna adds, as she comes back through from the kitchen. 'I think I might have made a bit of a pig of myself.'

I laugh, because I know that I ate far more than I should have. I seem to have acquired an appetite in the last few weeks now that I've rediscovered my love of cooking.

We leave the table and Deanna and I make ourselves comfortable on the sofa while Kayla kneels down on the floor by the Christmas tree and begins to pull the presents out from underneath. She surprises me by getting up and bringing a large, silver wrapped present over to me and placing it on the floor in front of me.

'Is that for me?' I ask, in surprise.

'Yep.' She goes back to the tree and returns with another two gifts and I see from the neatly handwritten tags that they're from Douglas and Prue. One of them looks suspiciously like a tin of biscuits. Prue buys me a tin of Marks and Spencer's finest every year and I can't complain because they're very nice. Kayla then puts hers and Deanna's gifts on the floor in front of the sofa and armchair.

Once we're all seated, Kala looks at me expectantly.

'You first,' she says. 'The big one.'

I pull the gift towards me. It's rectangular and

about three feet high and two foot wide. It feels like a picture frame. I begin to tear the paper away and when it's all off I stare in amazement at the painting in front of me. The canvas is a mass of vibrant colours and the paint appears to have been mixed with something as it has an almost three-dimensional effect to it.

In one corner of the picture there's an explosion of colour that seems to burst outwards from the canvas, I immediately recognise this as the corner of my garden where my colourful heathers are. The colours gradually merge into the green of the lawn and then in the middle of the painting is the brown trunk of the flowering cherry. The tree doesn't flower until May or June but Kayla has used poetic licence and painted starbursts of bright pink coming from the branches. She's captured it perfectly. I look up to see that Kayla is staring at me intently.

'Thank you,' I say quietly. 'It's absolutely beautiful. You have such talent.'

'You like it?' Kayla asks, hesitantly. 'I know it's not summer but I thought it would be a shame not to paint the tree in flower. We've got one in our back garden and it's so pretty.'

'It's perfect,' I say, wiping a tear from my eye. 'It's the best Christmas present that I've ever had.'

The expression on Kayla's face is one of pure delight and I'm touched by how many hours this must have taken her to paint. She has no way of knowing that I planted the flowering cherry in memory of Stephanie and that it's bloomed every year since her death without fail.

'It's from Mum as well,' Kayla says. 'She got it framed for you.'

The frame is black and glossy and goes perfectly with the painting, making the colours spring from the canvas.

'Thank you, Deanna,' I say. 'It's a fabulous frame.'

Deanna smiles and I think what a generous-hearted woman she is; I've hijacked her Christmas and her daughter; most people would be miffed about that but she's been kindness itself.

'It can go above the fireplace,' I say, looking up at the large, ornate mirror that's hung on the wall for as long as I remember.

'Don't feel you have to hang it there,' Kayla says. 'I won't be offended if you put it on a bedroom wall or something.'

'Absolutely not!' I say. 'It's having pride of place because it's brilliant and deserves to be seen. I love it.'

Kayla beams and I sneak a glance at Deanna's face; she looks so proud.

'Now,' I say. 'It's time you both opened your presents from me.'

Deanna goes first and professes delight at the boxed collection of pampering potions and lotions that I've given her. Kayla told me that Deanna loves to be pampered but rarely buys anything for herself as she can't afford it. She stares at me in disbelief as she opens the envelope that I'd tucked inside the box.

'A spa day?' she asks, in delight. 'You've given me an actual spa day! How wonderful.'

'It's for two,' I say. 'So you can take a friend.'

'I'll come!' shouts Kayla.

Deanna laughs and I join in. Deanna puts the voucher back in the envelope and carefully tucks it back into the box.

'Thank you, she says, quietly. 'And not just for the present but for looking after Kayla, I can't thank you enough.'

I'm prevented from answering by a loud squeal. Kayla has ripped the paper from her present and is staring at the contents.

'OMG,' she squeals. 'I can't believe you've got me this! How did you even *know*? She's holding the lid of the large wooden storage box open and staring inside at the contents. I didn't know but I asked someone who did. I went into the only art shop in the county and asked what the perfect present would be for an artist. The owner assured me that the box contained pretty much everything that a painter could ever need and to make doubly sure, there's a voucher underneath the tray of water colours so that Kayla can buy whatever else she wants.

'Thank you so much,' Kayla says.

'You're welcome,' I say. 'And don't forget, all of the paints and equipment upstairs are yours too.'

Kayla stares at me for a moment and then jumps up from her seat and bounds towards me. She leans over and flings her arms around me and hugs me tightly.

'You're going to be sick of my paintings,' she says, as she releases me from her hold and straightens up. 'You're going to run out of walls to hang them on!'

She laughs and Deanna and I join in.

This is what Christmas should be like.

CHAPTER EIGHTEEN

There's a laundry service on the ship where you leave everything in a bag and it's returned washed and ironed the next day – or I can take my clothes to the passengers' launderette and wash them myself. I've decided to treat myself and use the laundry service because it's not like I can't afford it and I am on holiday. I don't much fancy having to hang around a launderette waiting for a washing machine cycle to finish when there'll be lots of activities onboard that I want to join in.

I have three large suitcases that are packed to bursting point along with a smaller holdall containing my makeup and toiletries. It seems a ridiculous amount of clothes to take with me but the cruise is for four months and I don't want to be wearing the same outfits over and over again. I thought I'd overdone it but as we drive along the dockside I look around at the people waiting to board and they seem to have far more cases than me so I think that I've been quite restrained. Quite honestly, I don't know how some of them are going to fit it all into their cabins.

I've booked an outside cabin – or rather stateroom, as the cruise line rather grandly calls it – with a balcony. I've splashed out and gone for a deluxe stateroom so there should be plenty of room for me as the cabin is really for two people and there's only one of me.

Douglas has insisted on driving me to Southampton even though I told him that I was happy to get a taxi. Thankfully, Prue couldn't come as she had to work today.

Is that unkind of me, to not want her here? It probably is but I don't care; I don't want her sour face to spoil the start of my world cruise. She wouldn't be able to stop herself from making cutting comments and I don't want to embark on my holiday feeling rattled by her miserable face. Prue has made it quite clear that she doesn't approve of my decision to take a cruise and she's obviously annoyed that Douglas is refusing to side with her. I must admit that I was surprised that he's not agreed with Prue because I fully expected him to. He's gone up in my estimation in recent weeks and I'm realising that he's not the man that I took him for.

The car slows and Douglas pulls in smoothly

behind a large Landover type vehicle and parks neatly behind it.

'It's well big, that ship,' Kayla remarks from the back seat. I turn to see her staring at the dockside in fascination, her nose pressed against the car window.

'It is,' I say, as I turn and study the ship through the window. The ship looks far, far bigger in reality than it did in the brochure. It's almost scarily big.

'Well, here we are, Auntie Ria,' Douglas says, as he turns the ignition off. 'This is where your big adventure begins.'

It is indeed.

Douglas turns towards me and looks at me intently for a moment before opening the door and clambering out.

I take a deep breath, open the door and get out of the car and stand and look at the ship. Kayla climbs out from the back seat and stands next to me, stamping her furry-booted feet and tucking her hands underneath her armpits. The day is bitterly cold with a definite hint of more snow in the air and as we breathe out plumes of vapour blow into the air. The weather has been extremely cold for weeks now and the thought of warmth and sunshine is appealing.

We stand and watch as the porters scuttle busily around the large car park loading luggage onto trolleys which they then push towards the ship. A steady trail of passengers are making their way from the drop-off area to the check-in terminal.

Douglas pulls my cases from the boot as if they weigh nothing and plonks them in a neat line in front of the car. He goes back and closes the boot and locks the car and returns to stand next to us. The three of us stand for a moment and stare at the ship before Douglas grasps the handle of a case in each hand and sets off towards the terminal building. Kayla and I follow behind, Kayla pulling a suitcase behind her while I carry my holdall. In his usual efficient manner Douglas manages to commandeer a porter almost instantly, and, boarding details imparted and luggage tags checked, my suitcases and holdall are loaded onto a trolley and whisked away. I wonder briefly whether anyone has ever embarked on their cruise without their luggage but dispel the thought; one case might go astray but surely not all three.

'I suppose I should go and check in,' I say, as my cases vanish out of sight.

Douglas and Kayla look at me and I stare back at them uncertainly, unsure what to do.

'Well, goodbye,' I say, sounding awkward and stilted.

Douglas stares at me intently for a moment before suddenly stepping forwards and wrapping his arms around me and enveloping me in a bear hug. He holds me tightly and I stand stiffly in absolute astonishment for several seconds before returning his embrace. Whatever I was expecting, it wasn't that.

'Have a fantastic time, Auntie Ria,' he says,

gruffly as he releases his hold on me. 'And make sure you come back refreshed and rejuvenated.' I stare up at him and realise that he's fighting back the tears.

Before I have a chance to reply Kayla flings her arms around me and hugs me tightly.

'You have fun,' she whispers against my hair. 'And make sure you WhatsApp me tons of pictures.'

'I will,' I manage to mumble.

I take a deep breath and put my shoulders back; it's time to check in.

'Goodbye you two,' I say. 'And thank you both for everything. You've been wonderful.' My voice breaks on the last word and I pull my lips into a wobbly smile and with a little wave, I set off towards the cruise terminal.

'Bon Voyage,' Kayla calls from behind me. 'See you in four months.'

I turn and smile and take one last look at them both.

'And it's au revoir, Auntie Ria, not goodbye,' Douglas calls from behind me. 'You'll be back before you know it.'

If only that were true.

CHAPTER NINETEEN

After George's confession I found that I couldn't look at him without thinking you lied to me for forty-three years. *On the surface our life continued as it always had and if I acted any differently George never noticed, or commented.*

If George hadn't believed that he was dying he'd never have told me what he'd done.

I wished that he hadn't.

I'd accepted that Stephanie's death was my fault and come to terms with it and had found some sort of way of carrying on.

But now he'd confessed what he'd done he'd re-opened the wound and made it raw again; incredibly, his confession had made things worse, not better. I couldn't stop thinking about all of the lost years; all of the life that I'd wasted by blaming and absolutely hating myself. I'd lived with my guilt for so long that I now didn't know how to feel. Instead of being grateful that Stephanie's death wasn't completely my fault, I found that I couldn't find any sort of peace at all, just a dislike towards George that grew, day by day into hatred.

The hatred was as bad as the grief and I was slowly coming to the conclusion that I was going to have to leave him. I couldn't live with him any longer because I couldn't bear to look at him. I also knew that this time, I was going to get help; I was going to get some counselling so that I could come to terms with George's lie.

It was time to make a life for myself.

But events conspired against me; I didn't have to leave George because he had another heart attack before I could do so.

I was in the en-suite having a shower when he had his heart attack and when I came out into the bedroom he was lying across the bed, dead. Everyone agreed that it was a terrible shock for me and if only it had happened elsewhere or I hadn't been taking a shower, maybe George could have been saved.

But I'd lied.

The truth was that when I came out of the bathroom George was very much alive; he was lying on the bed clutching his chest and I knew straight away that he was having another heart attack. I ran over to him and stared down at him in a panic and then turned to the bedside table to pick up the telephone receiver to call for an ambulance.

But I didn't move.

I looked at George and somehow, I couldn't seem to make myself do it. I knew that I should call for an ambulance but I couldn't make my hands actually do it. George was looking up at me in shock and I found myself looking down at him dispassionately. I felt nothing for him; nothing at all and as I stared down at him all that was going through my mind was that I'd spent the last forty-three years living a half-life; a non-life because I couldn't forgive myself for killing our daughter. I remembered the many times that I'd sobbed in George's arms and told him how sorry I was, how I wished I could turn back the clock, how much I blamed myself, how much I hated myself.

And each time he'd held me and told me that I mustn't blame myself; that Stephanie's death was a terrible accident and that he didn't blame me and that I had to learn to forgive myself.

And all the time he knew.

So, to my shame, I watched him die.

And the only thing I felt was relief.

Relief that I'd never have to look at him again.

CHAPTER TWENTY

Three months later

The offices of Murray & Hepher Solicitors & Commissioners for Oaths are over a hundred years old; as old as the company itself. The office is spacious and has a comforting and timeless appeal to it, although the man seated behind the solid oak desk imparting the contents of Maria Simmonds last will and testament isn't old. A combination of fine blond hair and baby smooth skin conspires to make John Hepher look nearer to twenty-five than his real age of thirty-seven years.

When he's finished speaking there's a deathly silence in the room and the four people seated in front of his desk stare at him in bewilderment. The silence is eventually broken by Prue, who directs a glare at Kayla before turning her attention to John

Hepher.

'Obviously' she states. 'There has been some sort of mistake.'

Three pairs of eyes turn to look at Prue, the shock on Prue's face mirrored in their own.

'Would you like me to read it through again?' John Hepher asks.

'Yes. I think you'd better,' Prue says. 'I must have misheard.'

'Okay.' John Hepher clears his throat and begins to speak. He reads from the papers in front of him although in fact he knows the contents of this will off by heart. He drew up the will and had several long meetings with Maria Simmonds to ensure that it was exactly what she wanted.

'...to Kayla Winters I leave my house and the contents therein. If she inherits before the age of twenty-five the house is to be placed in trust for her until she reaches the age of twenty-five and until that time she cannot sell it. I also leave her the sum of fifty-thousand pounds. To my nephew...'

'I can't believe it,' Kayla whispers to Deanna, unable to stop the beginnings of a smile breaking out on her face.

'Really?' demands Prue, turning to Kayla and glaring at her. 'You knew Auntie Ria barely a matter of weeks and she leaves her house and money to you. Are we expected to believe that you didn't cajole and persuade her to change her will?'

'But I never knew, I mean I didn't think...' the

smile slides from Kayla face and she now looks close to tears.

'There is,' Prue states loudly, pointing her finger at Kayla. 'A name for people like you and it's not a nice one. I see it all of the time in my job and quite frankly, it disgusts me that people will befriend a vulnerable person solely to get their grubby hands on their money.'

'That's enough, Prue,' Douglas says quietly.

'I don't think I've said nearly enough...'

Douglas frowns at her and she stops talking and sits back in her chair with a sigh. She folds her arms across her body and presses her lips tightly together.

'Would you like me to continue?' John Hepher asks.

'Please,' Douglas says.

'Okay. To my nephew Douglas Simmonds, I leave the remainder of my estate after other minor bequests and taxes and duties have been paid. This amounts to two-hundred-and-ten-thousand-pounds and is made on condition that he does not, either at the time of my death, or at any time in the future, contest my will. If he should do so then the entire estate will revert to Kayla Winters.'

'Of course we're going to contest it!' Prue interrupts. 'This is ridiculous! She wasn't in her right mind when she made that will and a court will prove it. That house is ours and I'm not going allow a perfect stranger to steal it.'

John Hepher sighs and looks up from his desk. 'I

can assure you that Mrs Simmonds was of sound mind,' he says, calmly. 'And I would caution you to think very carefully before instigating legal action as contesting a will is a lengthy and costly process. Although, of course, you're perfectly entitled to seek independent advice.'

'We most certainly will be seeking advice.' Prue's face has turned a most unattractive shade of red, vastly different from her usual white pallor. 'It's quite obvious she wasn't of sound mind; she left her house to a stranger and never even told us she had cancer! If it wasn't for the hospital letters we'd never have known. And as for taking off on a world cruise and jumping overboard...'

There's a gasp from Kayla, and Deanna puts her arm around her and pulls her towards her. Douglas frowns at Prue.

'Sorry,' Prue says, not sounding sorry at all.

'I would remind you, Mrs Simmonds, that the coroner's verdict was accidental death,' John Hepher says, solemnly. 'A person lost overboard from a cruise ship is not as uncommon as you might think and the ship *was* in the midst of a tropical storm. There was nothing to suggest that Mrs Simmonds intended to take her own life; the very opposite, in fact, according to her fellow travellers.'

'That's true,' Kayla says. 'She was having a brilliant time and loving it because she sent me loads of photos and stuff about the places she was going to. And she'd made lots of new friends.'

'Well I don't care what texts she sent, I know she

wasn't thinking straight – she hadn't been right since Uncle George died.' Prue states. 'We will contest the will and we will win because no court in the land is going to agree with what she's done. So don't get too comfortable in that house, young lady.'

'We're not contesting the will,' Douglas says, quietly.

Prue turns to stare at him in astonishment.

'You're in shock, Doug, but I'm sure that when you've had time to think about it you'll change your mind. I have absolutely no intention of letting that girl walk away with...'

'Shut up, Prue,' Douglas interrupts.

'Douglas!' Prue says, sternly. 'How dare you speak...'

'SHUT. UP,' Douglas says again, loudly.

Prue opens her mouth to speak but closes it again when she sees the grim look on Douglas's face.

'I will *not* contest the will,' Douglas says. 'We already have a house and we don't need another one.'

'But that was Uncle George's house,' Prue says, in a wheedling tone. 'He would have wanted you to have it.'

'The house belonged to Auntie Ria,' Douglas says. 'Besides, what do we want another house for? We already have one. Auntie Ria has been very generous and left us a pile of money that we don't even need.'

Prue looks uncomfortable and places her hand

on Douglas's arm.

'Let's talk about it when we get home,' Prue says. 'We've all had a bit of a shock.'

Douglas shakes her hand off and crosses his arms.

'You never did like Auntie Ria,' he says, glaring at her.

'That's not true!' Prue says, widening her eyes in shock.

'Yes it is,' Douglas says. 'You always treated her as if she were a dimwit. Anyway, I'll decide what I'm going to do with the money because she left it to me, not you.'

Prue gasps and her hand flies to cover her mouth. Douglas has never spoken to her like this before.

'I may give it all to charity,' Douglas says calmly, crossing his legs. 'I'm sure Auntie Ria would approve.'

There's an uncomfortable silence in the room, broken by the sound of John Hepher clearing his throat. All four pairs of eyes look towards him, grateful for his interruption.

'So that completes the will reading,' he says. 'Aside from three bequests of a thousand pounds to local charities and five thousand pounds to Mr and Mrs Davies of 29 Fairview...'

'Mr and Mrs Davies?' Prue begins, before hurriedly closing her mouth when Douglas glares at her.

'Yes,' John Hepher says. 'The next door neighbours.'

'That's a bit of a surprise,' Douglas says, slowly. 'I didn't realise she knew them so well.'

'Oh, yes,' Kayla says. 'She got quite friendly with them. I think she felt sorry for them when they lost their dog.' She tucks her left hand underneath her right, crossing her fingers to negate the lie.

'Well, I'm astounded,' Prue says, unable to keep her mouth shut for more than a minute. 'It just shows that you can never really know what's going on in people's minds even though you've been close to them for years.'

'That's very true, Prue.' Douglas directs a level look at her. 'Sometimes, you suddenly realise that someone isn't the person that you always thought they were.'

Prue looks uncomfortable; she's not quite sure what Douglas is referring to but has a horrible feeling that he's getting at her. She remains silent and directs her gaze at the floor.

John Hepher begins to speak again, detailing the process of probate and the execution of the will. There's a subdued atmosphere in the room and when he's finished the four of them file from the room in silence and spill out onto the street.

After an awkward few minutes standing on the pavement in silence, Kayla and Deanna say a hesitant goodbye to Douglas and try to ignore the fact that Prue has turned her back to them and is ignoring them. Douglas watches as they walk down the high street towards the bus station and thinks that he should really have offered them a lift. He only stopped himself from doing so because he didn't want them to witness what he knows will be an unpleasant conversation with Prue in the car.

He pulls his mobile phone from his pocket and scrolls through the photographs.

'What are you looking at?' Prue demands, turning to face him.

'Pictures that Auntie Ria sent from the cruise.'

'Pictures? What pictures?' Prue asks. 'I didn't know she sent you pictures. How can you have had them all this time and not shown them to me?'

'Because you never asked,' Douglas says, quietly.

Prue frowns and glares at him.

'Actually,' Douglas says, aware that once he's spoken, it can never be unsaid. 'You never *ask* anything. You demand, you insist, you question, you command. But you never actually *ask*.'

Prue stares up at him, aware that something has changed and for once, she has no idea what to say.

Without speaking, Douglas turns his phone screen towards her, showing her the last picture that Ria sent. Ria is standing in the middle of a group of people all raising a glass of champagne to the camera. Wearing a sapphire blue, floor length evening dress, Ria looks radiant. She looks nothing at all like the Ria that Douglas had known since he was a child.

'She looks so different,' Prue says in disbelief. 'Younger. And glamorous. I hardly recognise her.'

'She looks nothing like the Auntie Ria that we know,' Douglas says.

'She doesn't,' Prue manages to stutter.

'But most of all,' Douglas says, with a smile. 'She looks happy.'

THE END

Thank you so much for reading this book, I really do appreciate it. I do hope that you've enjoyed it and if you have, please leave a review or star rating on Amazon/and or Goodreads.

Printed in Great Britain
by Amazon